Look for Omar's other adventures!

PLANET OMAR
INCREDIBLE RESCUE MISSION

ZANIB MIAN

ILLUSTRATED BY
NASAYA MAFARIDIK

putnam

G. P. PUTNAM'S SONS

G. P. PUTNAM'S SONS
An imprint of Penguin Random House LLC, New York

First published in Great Britain by Hodder and Stoughton, 2020
First American edition, 2021
First paperback edition published 2023
Text copyright © 2021 by Zanib Mian
Illustrations copyright © 2021 by Nasaya Mafaridik

Excerpt from *Planet Omar: Epic Hero Flop* text copyright © 2022 by Zanib Mian
Illustrations copyright © 2022 by Kyan Cheng

G. P. Putnam's Sons is a registered trademark of Penguin Random House LLC.
Penguin Books & colophon are registered trademarks of Penguin Books Limited.

Visit us online at penguinrandomhouse.com.

THE LIBRARY OF CONGRESS HAS CATALOGED THE HARDCOVER EDITION.
LC Number: 2021289557

Printed in the United States of America
ISBN 9780593109298

1st Printing
LSCH

Design by Suki Boynton
Text set in Averia Serif Libre

This book is dedicated to

all the children who do what's right,

even when nobody is looking.

OMAR

I have a secret collection of buttons nobody knows about (except you, you obviously know now because I wrote it here)

Can lick my elbow (can you?)

Scared of Pigeons >-<

I want to be on the first trip to Mars for people who aren't astronauts

BEEP.

BEEP,

BEEP,

BEE

CHAPTER 1

EEEEP!

That was my annoying alarm clock, waking me up for the first day of school after winter break. I didn't want to get up because I had been sleeping until at least nine o'clock for the last two weeks, so seven o'clock felt like practically the

MiddLe
of The NiGhT!

What was most annoying was that Mom had put it on the other side of the room instead of on my nightstand so I'd HAVE to get out of bed to turn off the beeps. Of course, I didn't want to, so I threw my pillow at it. The pillow was too heavy and fat or something, so it didn't get very far. I rummaged in my nightstand drawer for something else to throw and found a squishy ball I had kept because it smelled like

delicious
BUBBLE GUM.

I squinted at the clock and lifted the ball up . . .

READY, AIM, THROW!

Yikes. Just then, my sister, Maryam, was

walking into the room, saying,

"Turn that thing off, you lazy egg!"

GASP

Yep, you guessed it. She got hit right in the nose. Lucky it was squishy, or I would have gotten in TONS of trouble.

Needless to say, the rest of

the morning did not go smoothly. Mom and Dad weren't very impressed, and Maryam was super melodramatic about it, saying she wasn't ever going to talk to me again. Then my little brother, Esa, refused to put his coat on, which made us late, and everyone got even angrier. I was the only one in a good mood, because I couldn't wait to see my best friends, Charlie and Daniel.

They ran up to me on the playground and both gave me a slap on the back. A slap on the back is basically code for:

" Hey! I'm so happy to see you. I kind of missed you."

The slap is less cheesy than actually saying it,

SUPER OBVIOUSLY.

"Guess what," said Daniel. "My mom and dad finally got me a new bike! It's so cool. I can't wait to show it to you!"

"Ah. Lucky!" said Charlie.

"Yeah, the chain still keeps falling off when I ride mine," I said.

"Isn't your dad really good at fixing stuff?" asked Daniel.

"Yeah, he is—I should ask him.

The only thing he can't fix is Maryam,"

I said. And we all laughed and agreed about that.

We couldn't stop talking as we lined up on the playground for Mrs. Hutchinson to come

get us. I had brought her a

chocolate cupcake

from the stash my neighbor Mrs. Rogers

had brought over for us the day before.

Mrs. Hutchinson is probably the nicest

teacher ever. I mean, duh, nobody on the

entire planet would give one of their Mrs.

Rogers' cupcakes to somebody they didn't

like. I thought Mrs. Hutchinson deserved

one, for the winks she gave us at the right

moments, for always being fair when two

kids got into a fight and for the

fun way she taught us.

Before winter break, we'd been
doing a project about the
universe, and she told us
about how some scientists
believe there is life
on other planets.

Basically, that means
aliens, so Mrs.

Hutchinson got us to
imagine what they might
look like—it wasn't really
like a lesson at all!

"Be careful, though," she had said.
"They might be watching us. We
don't want them to know we are
onto them."

But that morning, when a teacher came to bring us in, it wasn't Mrs. Hutchinson.

It was someone **taller** and **thinner** and with way **less fun hair.**

She had the kind of creases in her face that told me she had spent most of her life frowning and furrowing her eyebrows. Her clothes were gray and her shoes were POINTY. The way less fun hair was pulled so tightly and so

neatly into a bun
that I imagined
she'd needed the
help of a high-tech
laser that detected
any out-of-place
hairs and zapped
them down.

Daniel and
Charlie looked
at me with their
question-mark
eyebrows. Have
you ever noticed
that the eyebrows
say the most about
someone's feelings?

For example, Charlie's eyebrows can say:

EH? WHAT'S GOING ON?

Most often seen when he is doing one of his math problems.

WOW, THIS IS SO FUN!

Most often seen when we have discovered a new game to play.

OMG, I'M GOING TO DIE.

Most often seen when a spider crawls up the wall.

Anyway, back to the strange teacher.

Eerily, the only thing she said to us was "Follow me." And she spun around on the sharpest heel I have ever seen and walked toward the school building.

CHAPTER 2

We piled into the classroom and went to our desks.

"Who IS this?" whispered Daniel.

"Don't worry, it's probably nobody. Mrs. Hutchinson's probably just sick or something and she'll be back tomorrow," I said.

But just then, the new teacher said,

"I'm Mrs. Crankshaw. I will be your teacher for the rest of the school year."

She said those words from her mouth. But it felt like each word was a heavy metal object hitting me over the head.

I looked at Charlie. He had scared eyebrows. I wanted to put my arm around him.

Daniel was pinching my leg under the desk.

"Daniel! Stop it. Ouch! What are you doing?"

"I'm pinching you to make sure I'm not dreaming."

"YOU'RE SUPPOSED TO PINCH YOURSELF, SILLY!"

"You two at the back. Stop your nonsense," said Mrs. Crankshaw. "That brings me to my first task—assigning you all to your new seats. From now on, you will not sit next to your chatty little friends, you will sit where I say."

Gulp.

"She's not a nobody," said Daniel.

"No," I said. I looked down at the cupcake. It looked sad, too.

We had to
hold in all of
our questions and
emotions until break
time. None of us dared to
put our hand up and ask what
had happened to Mrs. Hutchinson.

Especially after my new seat neighbor,
Ellie, asked if she could do something as
innocent as get up and throw her pencil
shavings in the garbage, and she got
a LOOk that could
have made
Superman
poop his pants.

When we were released for recess, Charlie, Daniel and I did some super-fast speed walking toward the exit, because we aren't allowed to run.

All of us buttoned up our lips until the fresh, cold outside air hit our faces, and then Daniel practically exploded.

"Where's Mrs. Hutchinson?" he wailed.

Charlie just stood there looking at us, not saying anything. He seemed to be in shock.

"So it's not just for a day. She said she was our teacher *for the rest of the year*!" I said.

"But what happened to Mrs. Hutchinson? Why would she just leave us?!" asked Daniel.

"I don't know. But we have to find out."

I put my arm around Charlie, who still hadn't said anything. We couldn't lose Mrs. Hutchinson *and* Charlie both in the same day!

Finally, Charlie spoke. "Should we ask one of the other teachers?"

"Good idea," I said, already running toward the teacher on duty in the playground. Charlie and Daniel followed close behind.

Mr. Henry already had several children around him. He was scolding one of them while another stood there crying and others watched.

We waited for him to finish shouting, and then I said, "Mr. Henry, where is Mrs. Hutchinson?"

The teacher looked in all four directions to figure out where the question was coming from. He didn't realize it was from me, because about six other kids were still staring at him.

"I don't know! In the bathroom probably! Really, how should I know?" he said, rubbing his forehead as if it would make everyone go away.

Charlie tugged at my sleeve. "Come on, this isn't working."

We walked around the playground, not really saying much, which was fine by me, because my mind was busy imagining all the things that could have happened.

Maybe Mrs. Hutchinson had too many of those very light cheese puffs she eats every lunchtime, and they made her weightless, so she floated off into the clouds. Then I imagined that she somehow became invisible and was trying to get everyone's attention to help her come back down, but we just couldn't see her anymore.

"Mrs. Hutchinson! If you're there, throw a ball at us!" I said out loud.

"What?" said Charlie.

"Have you gone nuts?" said Daniel.

I giggled.

"It was worth a try..."

CHAPTER 3

On the way home, I told Mom all about the terrible disappearance of Mrs. Hutchinson.

"I'm sure there's a reasonable explanation," Mom said. "They'll probably send us a letter about it."

She was being very grown-up, obviously because she is a grown-up, but it was unhelpful and SUPER BORING.

I said, "But, Mom! What if something has happened to her and we need to launch a rescue mission?"

Mom rolled her eyes at me and said, "Hey, Siri, when do children stop overreacting to everything?"

Siri said, "I found this on the web."

Siri was Mom's best friend these days.

I rolled my eyes
back at Mom

and figured Maryam might be more helpful.

o o o

Maryam was lying on her bed when I got

home, tapping away on her phone.

"WOW!

You actually remembered to knock.
You must want something."

"Sort of. Mrs. Hutchinson is gone, and we
have a horrible teacher called Mrs. Crankshaw,
and Mom won't listen to me about it."

"Oh. Where has she gone?"

"Well, that's the thing. Nobody knows."

"Not right, Omar. Somebody knows.
You just have to find the somebody."

"Where do I find the somebody?"

"Probably the staff room. The staff room is full of G⬭SSIP and SeCReTS. That's why kids aren't allowed in there."

"Wow. Really?"

"Yes, really."

"OK, thanks!"

" Whatever, beaver breath."

I walked away, trying to smell my own breath, just to make sure.

I imagined what the staff room looked like. None of my friends had ever seen it. But I guessed it would be dark and lined with dusty files, all containing terrible secrets. I imagined the teachers taking their masks off when they went in, and all of them were ACTUALLY WITCHES, except Mrs. Hutchinson ... Maybe *that's* why they got rid of her?!

I ran downstairs to see if I could get Mom to listen to me again, but I got distracted by the bananas and chips she'd put on the table for a snack. She said I could only have the chips if I had a banana first, which is the only reason I had a banana, because I don't really like them unless they have the brown freckles all over, which means they are

soft and sweet inside.

It turned out the snacks were a trap—like honey for a bear . . .

"Please help Esa with his homework before you run off and disappear into your room, Omar," Mom said while I had my mouth full of banana.

"Mmmmmmm . . . !"

I tried to wriggle out of it by saying, "He never listens to me anyway."

"Yes he does."

"No he doesn't."

"Yes he does," said Esa, which made me laugh.

I was only complaining because I wanted to get back to thinking about what we could do about Mrs. Hutchinson. But how long could a three-year-old's baby homework take? Plus, last time I helped Esa, Dad let me choose what he would cook for dinner, which was cool. I chose spaghetti Bolognese because, like I always say, Dad's is the best.

"Come on, Esa," I said. "Let's do it in the living room."

The homework was to color in two shapes

that were the same in each row on a worksheet.
I could have done it in exactly thirty-eight
seconds, and believe me, I was tempted to do it
in a scribbly way and just pretend that Esa did
it, but I was worried he would tell Mom, and
even if he didn't,

Allah would super obviously know about it and He wouldn't be very proud of me.

So I sat with Esa for thirty minutes to help him
finish it, which is almost fifty times slower
than I would have been. Sheesh.

In my head, I was imagining a new
scientific breakthrough in medicine that

would make toddlers faster at everything. *Everyone* would want to buy that. I would make millions.

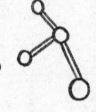

I decided I might have to pay more attention to what my scientist parents say all the time so I can get super good at it and make the medicine when I grow up a bit.

As we were finishing, Dad came home with his motorcycle helmet still on his head, which I always think makes him look a bit like an alien.

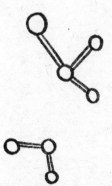

Esa ran up and jumped into his arms. I gave him a kiss on his helmet, and he said,

"zorgle borg,

what a welcome is this! Take me to your leader,

Earthlings."

We giggled at that, but it reminded me of Mrs. Hutchinson's alien lesson again, and my tummy turned over thinking about going back to school with Mrs. Crankshaw.

CHAPTER 4

The next day at school, we all sat in the seats
Mrs. Crankshaw had chosen for us. Charlie
was near me, but Daniel was across the room.
My seat was next to Ellie's. She was OK, but

definitely not as fun
as sitting right next to
one of my best friends. ☺

Charlie was close enough to try to talk to,

but that got me lots of angry LOOKS from Mrs. Crankshaw.

She was teaching us about how people lived in medieval times. She wasn't making history fun, like Mrs. Hutchinson would. It was as if she was trying to make it boring. Maybe she had a "making things boring" super-villain power.

I bet she could even make Ferraris sound boring.

I wanted desperately to tell Charlie so we could both laugh about it, but Mrs. Crankshaw had her eyes on me. Ellie suggested that if I wanted to say something to Charlie, I could whisper it to her, and she would whisper it to Sarah, who would whisper it to Jason, who would whisper it to Charlie.

I agreed that was a good plan and
whispered, **"This is boring."**

I watched as the girls passed my words
along. Charlie understood what was going
on and was grinning his toothy grin in
anticipation.

When it finally got to him, he said, "What?

chris is Snoring??

No he isn't!"

I face-palmed at the complete flop. If I was
going to stop myself from falling asleep, I
needed to think more drastically . . .

I shot my hand up to ask if I could go to the
bathroom. **I didn't need to pee,
and before you think it,
no, I didn't need to p💩💩.
I had a plan.**

Surprisingly, Mrs. Crankshaw let me go.

I winked at Daniel on my way out.

I made my way down the hall in the opposite direction from the bathroom, looking over my shoulder in case Mrs. Crankshaw was following me. I  wondered what I would have done if I had turned around and seen her.

Pretended I was lost?

Or run? Or played dead?

(Hey, why not? It works for spiders!)

I arrived at my destination. You guessed it—the staff room.

I was hoping to bump into the *somebodies* who knew what was going on with Mrs. Hutchinson. I was in luck, because one of the second-grade teachers was coming toward me. She was walking the way Maryam does when she tries on a pair of Mom's heels for fun. It must have been the first time this teacher had worn heels, too.

I held my breath in case she yelled at me for being there, but to my relief, she smiled and asked, "How can I help you?"

"I, erm, wanted to ask if you know where Mrs. Hutchinson is?"

Her smile vanished. "Well, that's nosy, isn't it?

Don't worry, if the school wants you to know, you will know," she said. And then she walked into the staff room and closed the door behind her without even looking at me.

Wow, that was secretive, I thought. *Maybe a bit too secretive. Something suspicious is going on.*

I started running back toward my classroom and then saw the "no running" sign, so I switched to speed-walking instead. Then I realized nobody was around to  get me in trouble, so I switched to running again. Then I heard Dad's voice in my head, saying, **"Do what's right, even if nobody is looking,"** so I sighed and switched back to speed-walking. It's hard work being good sometimes.

I sat back down at my desk and quickly

scribbled a note to pass to Charlie:

CHAPTER 5

We were bursting to talk more at lunchtime, but we had to keep it in until we got to the playground after eating. That's because Sarah and Ellie were sitting right next to us in the cafeteria, and they were clearly in

EAVESDROPPING MODE.

Instead of talking to each other, they were just staring into space and smiling at each other now and then. Could they be any more obvious?

I wondered why they were so interested in us today. Usually they're chatting away about their own stuff . . .

I hoped they hadn't sneakily read the note I passed to Charlie! I figured if something was going on with Mrs. Hutchinson and the other teachers were in on it, then we had to keep it to ourselves until we knew more. It could be dangerous.

"Finally! We can talk!" I said as soon as we left the cafeteria.

"*Talk* already! What do you mean Mrs. Hutchinson is in trouble?" said Charlie, wiggling his eyebrows between excited and worried.

"What? When did this happen?" asked Daniel.

We told him I found out in medieval times,

which made us all laugh, even in this serious situation.

"I hate being at that faraway desk,

all the way in
Narnia,"

complained Daniel. "I'm going to be the last to find everything out!"

"OR you'll be the first, but you won't be able to tell us," said Omar.

"Even worse! You know I can't keep anything in."

"Yeah, we know," said Charlie, fanning the air around his nose.

"What? It's not my fault.

I had beans for lunch ..."

We walked away from the smell, relocating to a more hidden spot behind a tree. I explained to my friends what the second-grade teacher said to me. "You know what that means, don't you? They are hiding something. All the teachers.

First, Mr. Henry said that she was in the bathroom, and now this teacher is acting all suspicious and secretive."

"SeCReLy," corrected Charlie.

"I'm pretty sure it's 'secretive,' but we can go with 'secrety.'"

"So what are we going to do?" said Daniel.

"I think we should launch a

SEARCH MiSSiON.

But not inside the school," I said. "Because the teachers are clearly in on it—or they would have told us what's happened to her."

"What, like put missing posters up on lampposts?" asked Daniel.

"That's one idea, but we'll need to do more," I said.

"Maybe we could ask

LanCeLot MacIntosh.

He's her uncle, remember?" suggested

Charlie.

I did remember. Lancelot Macintosh is

Mrs. H's super-cool uncle, who drives a Ferrari

without showing off, and who supported us in

our save-the-mosque money-raising campaign.

"Yes! He should be the first one we talk to,"

I said.

We made a plan to make missing posters

using a photo of Mrs. Hutchinson from the

wall near the office, where there was a photo

of every member of staff in the school. Most

of them weren't smiling in their pictures; they **were very serious, or even miserable,** except Mrs. Hutchinson. She was smiling in hers, as if she had just seen a **baby UNICORN.** Every time I looked at the wall, it made me want to grab a marker and put smiles on everyone's faces, the way Maryam and I draw funny hats and mustaches on people in magazines.

"Daniel, would you mind bringing your phone in one day and taking a photo of her photo?"

I'm not allowed a phone of my own yet, even though lots of kids in my class have one, including Daniel. Mom and Dad say I can only get one when I am thirteen, which still feels like a million years away.

"I'm not allowed to use my phone at school..." started Daniel.

"Oh . . . yeah . . . hmmm."

"But you know I'm going to do it anyway!"

He giggled.

Charlie and I giggled, too, but I was hoping this mission wouldn't land any of us in trouble.

CHAPTER 6

After school, I went over to see our next-door neighbor Mrs. Rogers, because she always has the best cookies and listens to all my worries without saying they are nothing to worry about.

"This is definitely very suspicious,"

she said after I finished telling her everything. And I loved her for it. "You could use The Facebook to try to find her.

Apparently, you can write on The Facebook and the whole world can see it. My son John signed me up on it from his computer, which was nice, but I have to wait to use his computer again to look at it, because he didn't sign me up on mine."

I pushed a giggle back into my mouth because I didn't want Mrs. Rogers to think I was laughing at her.

"That's not how the internet works, Mrs. Rogers. You can sign in to your Facebook account from any computer, anywhere in the world."

"Oh really? That is fascinating, isn't it?"

"Sort of." I grinned.

"Well, the first step is to go and poke around the area she lives in. Bet you'll find

around there."

"I know exactly which road she lives on,

because I saw her carrying in her groceries once when Dad and I were driving past!"

"Fantastic. That makes things a lot easier. Get your dad to take you back, and then let me know how it goes," said Mrs. Rogers with a wink. "And say hi to your mom. Tell her I haven't had a biryani in a while."

BIRYANI

"Umm, we sent you some last weekend, Mrs. Rogers."

"Like I said, it's been too long!"

I giggled and promised I would ask Mom to make some more of her favorite Pakistani food.

When we first moved in next door to Mrs. Rogers, she hated the smell of our food cooking.

But now that she's more part of our family, she gets excited by the smell, knowing what's going to hit her taste buds.

My dad told us that once, when he took a chickpea curry for lunch to his lab, all his colleagues thought that the smell was one of their experiments gone wrong. He was super embarrassed until he let everyone taste it and they all went mad for the yummy flavor.

I walked the few steps back to my house, but I took my time because I heard a whizzing noise from above. I looked up at the sky, where I could see nothing but clouds. But what was the sound? I imagined it was an alien spaceship, hiding behind the clouds. Which made me wonder . . . what if Mrs. H was in an alien spaceship? It wasn't impossible . . . After all, she was the one who said there were aliens up there!

When I opened the front
door, Esa was unfolding all
of the fresh laundry
Mom had just done and
flinging it across the room.
"It's sn❄wing!"
He grinned happily.
I jumped around trying to grab socks
and T-shirts from places high
and low. "Stop it, Esa. Mom
will be super angry with you."

Just then, Mom walked into the room with her cup of coffee in hand. **"For the love of rectangles!"** she blurted out. **Mom is so random.**

She walked straight back out, mumbling something about at least getting to finish a cup of coffee before it got cold.

I folded the laundry again as well as I could. It's not as easy as it looks!

Then I used my very best puppy-dog eyes and asked Maryam if I could use her phone to call Charlie and Daniel.

"Get ready," I told them. **"We're going on a <u>mission</u>, tomorrow after school, on our bikes..."**

CHAPTER 7

The next day, we could barely focus on
our already-boring work in class. We were
dying for school to be over so we could keep
searching for Mrs. Hutchinson.

Mrs. Crankshaw had to deal with her first
class incident when Sarah tripped over Daniel's
big boots and fell, hitting her head on the side of
a desk. There was blood, right near her eyebrow.
It wasn't pretty and I was really
worried about her, especially
because she was wailing very loudly.

But Mrs. Crankshaw went over and looked at Sarah as if nothing had happened. As if she had no blood trickling down her cheek. "OK. You can go to the nurse," she said. And *then* she put her hands over her ears so she wouldn't be able to hear the crying.

It made me miss Mrs. Hutchinson even more. She couldn't hide how worried she got when a kid hurt themselves, because

her springy curls would immediately lose their spring.

Mrs. Hutchinson would always send another child to the nurse with the person who had hurt themselves, just to make sure they were OK on the way.

"Oh, she's cranky for sure,"

said Charlie in a whisper, looking at all of us near his desk, the way he does when he makes a joke, like he's checking how funny it was.

We all laughed, which was a super-bad idea because, as if by some witchy magic, our new teacher appeared out of nowhere, piercing us with her eyes.

"And what exactly is so funny over here?" she demanded, looking at me. Probably because I was the one who

LAUGHED THE LOUDEST.

"Nothing," I said.

And before she spoke, I knew what she was going to say. The same thing all adults on the planet say when you say "nothing."

"It's obviously not nothing. It's something."

We all stared down at our hands in our laps, not daring to look up.

She crossed her arms and pursed her lips.

"Well, 'nothing' can cost you your recess. So be careful." She dropped this bomb as she spun around on her sharp heel and stormed off.

The class worked in silence for the rest of the day, but rumors were already starting to spread on the playground about Mrs. Crankshaw being a

SUPERVILLAIN

who had **escaped from a**

high-security jail

and disguised herself as a schoolteacher.

CHAPTER 8

After what seemed like forever, we were finally
together on our bikes. Charlie, Daniel and me.
Dad had actually managed to sort out my chain
problem. We met at our usual spot,
which we had figured out was an equal
distance from all three of our homes. If you
want to know how we did that, I'll tell you.
It was easy. We all left our own houses on
foot and counted our steps on the way.
Charlie had taken 215 steps, Daniel 189 and
me 192. We noticed that Charlie's steps are
smaller, so it was actually about the same

distance. Dad said that the whole thing

wasn't very °scientific° and he

raised one eyebrow. It was the eyebrow that

told me I should know better because I am

the son of two scientists.

BUT COME ON,

sometimes even I can't be bothered to do

PERFECT SCIENCE.

"All right, guys," I said, rubbing my hands together. "First stop, Mrs. Hutchinson's house. Follow me and be careful—it might be

A CRIME SCENE

that the police haven't discovered yet, so no touching anything. Except the doorbell. We'll have to touch the doorbell."

"But what if we leave **fingerprints** and then later the police think we did it?!" said Charlie.

"Does everyone have gloves?" Daniel asked.

Luckily we'd all remembered to bring them. So we put them on and sped off.

As we rode, Charlie said, "She might be at home. Maybe she just decided not to be our teacher anymore."

I thought about this in my head and said,

"No. Mrs. Hutchinson would never, ever do that."

But my heart was beating at the thought of her opening her front door. And when we got there and I went to press the doorbell, my hand was shaking.

BRRRRRING!

We waited. Charlie held on to the hood of my jacket for comfort, and Daniel held on to Charlie's arm. Which made me imagine myself at the circus, being the person on the bottom that all the other people stand and balance on. That person has to be the

STRONGEST,

to hold everyone up.
If I ran away now,
we would all run
away. So I tried to
remember to

breathe
slowly.

I conjured up my
imaginary dragon,
H_2O, who breathes
cool steam. I don't
imagine him very
often anymore, but I
needed him now, to
help me stay calm.

Nobody came

to the door, **which made me said and happy all at once**. Sad because that meant Mrs. Hutchinson *was* missing. But happy because it meant that she didn't just decide to stop being our teacher.

We rang it another couple of times and waited, to be triple super sure. Then we peeked in through the mail slot.

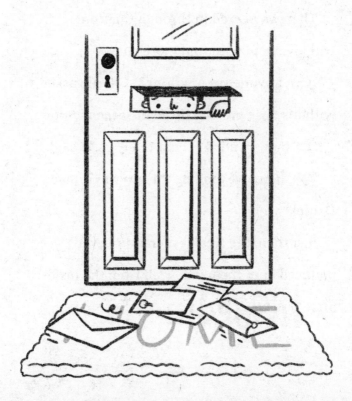

There was a whole pile of mail on the floor.

"You know what that means, don't you, guys?" I said quietly.

"She hasn't been home," Charlie gasped.

"For *days*!" Daniel added.

Then we peered in through the front window, hoping to find more clues.

"Can anyone see anything?" Charlie asked, with his nose pressed up against the window.

"Errmm . . . nooo . . . not really . . ." I said.

"What are we looking for, anyway?" said Daniel.

Just then, the freakiest creature ever pounced onto the windowsill from the inside and **hi$$ed!**

All three of us screamed and leaped backward onto the grass. Charlie practically jumped into Daniel's lap.

"Whaaaaat was that?"

he shrieked.

"I don't know. I've never seen anything like it!" I said.

"I think it was just a cat . . . *I think*," said Daniel.

"But it wasn't furry!"

Charlie was still shrieking. "Or cute!"

"Yeah, it was, like, just skin, yucky skin." I grimaced.

"Like an

iNSiDe-Out cat!"

Charlie said.

"Guys, what if it's an alien? Trying to disguise itself as a cat, but it doesn't quite know what cats look like? Or maybe its fur-disguise feature is out of order?!" I said, thinking back to the spaceship I had imagined in the clouds.

Charlie and Daniel stared at me blankly. None of us spoke for a long, awkward moment.

Just when I thought my friends thought my idea was way too crazy this time, Charlie said, "I mean, it was *really* weird-looking. I guess we shouldn't rule anything out—right, Daniel?"

"Oh, come on," he replied.

"You're supposed to be the clever one, Omar! Why would aliens steal Mrs. H and disguise themselves as a hairless cat?"

I sort of knew what Daniel meant, but I couldn't let go of my idea that easily. I looked  up at the sky again and then down at my feet. I noticed something very strange. We were standing in a circle of grass that was a completely different color from the grass around it.

I spun around to look at the rest of the grass and saw that there were four circles just like that, making a pattern on Mrs. H's front lawn.

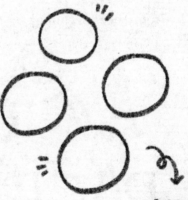

SPACESHIP LANDING SPOT?!

"Ermmm, guys, LOOK!" I pointed down.

"That's weird," said Charlie.

"Hmmm. What are those?" said Daniel.

They were really odd. Especially because the rest of Mrs. H's yard looked like somebody's very green fingers had been working on it, making it all pretty and neat.

"What can make weird circle patches like that?" asked Charlie.

In my head, I thought:

A SPACESHIP!

And I wanted to shout out: *A SPACESHIP,
GUYS!* But this time, I kept it to myself,
because Daniel thought my aliens idea was too
wacky.

"I think we should get out of here," I said,
grabbing my bike.

CHAPTER 9

We rode slowly back toward our houses,

talking about the evidence we had seen.

1. a pile of unread mail on the doormat
2. a weird creature at the window
3. weird markings on the grass

We decided that the first clue had to mean
that she had been kidnapped and had not been
home for a long time. **She must still
be with the captors!**

The other two clues were just weird. In
my head, they were definitely alien clues.
Charlie thought they could be, too, but
maybe he was just trying to be nice, because
then he said the most likely explanation was
that she had been kidnapped by humans.
Because humans were definitely more
common on Earth, mathematically there was
more chance of it being humans.

[charlie loves math.]

Daniel said there was no way it could be aliens,
and why were we distracting ourselves from
the real kidnappers with the idea? (This is why

it's good to have more than one best friend:
in case one of them thinks your imagination
has gotten out of control . . .)

"Should we tell our parents?" Charlie asked.

"NoOoOoOo WAY!"

said Daniel.

I thought about it. "Hmmm. They might be
able to help . . . but on the other hand, they
would absolutely hit the roof if they found out
that I had gone outside 'the perimeter'
on my bike. YIKES."

"The perimeter" is a very strict zone that
I am allowed to ride my bike in when I'm not
with Mom or Dad or Maryam. I had broken the
perimeter by *a lot* to try to save Mrs. H.

"I would never, ever, ever admit to my
parents how far we went from home," said

Daniel. "They're coming up with more and more genius punishments for me, like they've been reading a book about it."

"Haha, what? Like there's a book called *No Screen Time for a Week and Other Genius Punishments for Kids*." I laughed.

"No, no." Charlie giggled. "*209 Million Ways to Make Your Child Behave*."

"*How to Train Your Kids and Other Animals*," Daniel said, slapping his knee with delight.

"Seriously, though, it might be worth it, if they can help Mrs. H." I decided she was even worth losing Xbox time for a little while.

So that night, I casually walked into Mom and Dad's room, where they were reading in bed, even though it wasn't really bedtime yet. They had chosen

Geeky science books,

obviously. But a closer look at Dad's cover convinced me to tell them about our suspicions, because it was about the universe.

"What's up, darling?" asked Mom.

"Need batteries again?" said Dad.

Wow, how did he know that? I actually did need

batteries again, but I decided to use this time wisely and stick to the more important issue.

"No, I want to talk to you about Mrs. Hutchinson . . ."

"What about her? Is she back?" said Mom.

"No, that's what I want to talk about," I said, jumping onto the bed and **wriggling** myself a space right between them.

This was great—now I could say things without having to look them in the face.

"So . . . don't be mad, but . . ."

"You know when you start a sentence with **'DON'T BE MAD,'** we probably will be mad," said Mom.

"It's OK to tell us," said Dad. "Maybe we will just be a teeny bit mad."

I took a deep breath. "OK. Well, we had to find out what happened to her, so we rode our bikes to her house and saw some stuff."

"You r⊛de your bike outside the perimeter?!

OUTSIDE it? OUTside, as in the side you promised never to go on?" said Mom, holding her head in her hands as if it would blow away if she didn't.

"Yes, but—"

"No buts!"

"And what did you see, Omar?" said Dad, who wanted to hear the rest.

The whole scene reminded me of the good cop–bad cop thing that they talk about in movies.

"We saw that her mail, from many days, was in a massive pile on the doormat, so she's definitely missing."

"That doesn't mean she's missing. It just means she hasn't been home for a while," said Mom.

Dad nodded in agreement.

"Yes, but she would have said if she was going away, so it's really **SUSPICIOUS!**" I said. "Plus, we also saw some really weird stuff . . . which made me think it might be . . ."

"What? What might it be?" asked Dad.

"Well, I just *think* this, and it could be true . . ."

"Go on, spit it out."

"It might be an ALIEN abduction . . ."

Mom and Dad looked at each other really fast. I knew they must have made faces I couldn't see. They must have had their "oh dear" eyebrows on.

"It's not an alien abduction, sweetie," Mom said gently. "Because there's no such thing as aliens . . . OK?"

"Well, it depends how you define aliens," said Dad.

I perked up and looked at him. He was

Mom gave him a playful whack and said, "Stop encouraging him!" Then she said to me, "I'm sure Mrs. Hutchinson is perfectly fine, so please drop this nonsense. And as for you going outside the perimeter, I am very disappointed."

I let my head drop to show them I was sorry.

"I should really say that you can't go out on your bike unsupervised again," said Mom.

"But then your fitness would suffer." Dad finished her thoughts like he always does.

If they took away my bike rides, we wouldn't be able to continue our mission! I held my breath.

"Perhaps taking away screen time might be better," said Dad.

No°oo°oo°o.
Not my screen time!

I screamed in my head.

Out loud I said, "You could take away

vegetables from my meals for two weeks?"

"You wise guy watermelon!"

said Dad. "Do you think you have the right to

be a wise guy right now?" And he tickled me

without mercy until I said I might wet myself.

Then he said, "OK, then, Captain Wise Guy.

I'm proud of you for choosing to tell us all

this. But even though you had a heroic reason

for doing it, I hope you understand that it's

a very serious thing you've done. We put the

perimeter in place to keep you safe, because

we love you. Now you will have to face the

consequences of breaking the rules.

"Two weeks of no video games at all."

"OK . . ." I said. I knew it would be at least that, anyway.

"As for the alien abduction, I'm afraid Mom's right. Aliens have not taken Mrs. H. Just try to forget about it and wait and see what we hear."

"OK . . ." I said again. I climbed off Mom and Dad's bed and went to mope around in my own.

Of course they wouldn't believe us about the kidnapping, or alien abduction, or whatever was happening with Mrs. H. They were ADULTS without imaginations and they were boring most of the time. I wondered if my parents would have believed us if they were detectives instead of scientists. Detectives have to consider all the options, and they might even consider out-of-this-world ones, like my friends and I were. **We were being GOOD DETECTIVES.**

∘ ∘ ∘

When I told Charlie and Daniel how my parents reacted, we decided that it wasn't worth telling any more grown-ups. The school or the police wouldn't believe three elementary school kids any more than our own parents. And anyway, what if the school was covering something up, and telling the police would put Mrs. H in more danger when they started asking questions?

No. We had to get to the bottom of this ourselves.

We decided we'd go out to investigate more on Saturday.

CHAPTER 10

Friday-night dinner was chicken and mushroom pie. Mrs. Rogers was over, as she sometimes is for dinner, but she was disappointed the food was English.

YUM!

"English food is boring," she said, flicking off a stray flake of pastry from her purple cardigan. "I want chili and spice and all things nice."

Esa giggled at the rhyming words and attempted to shovel some pie onto his fork.

"Well, Mrs. Rogers, we're taking a family trip to Pakistan. There's lots of spicy food there—maybe you should come?" Dad joked.

"Oh, I'm past my days of getting on a long flight!" said Mrs. Rogers. "But you're welcome to bring some back for me!"

"Whaaaat? We're going to Pakistan?!"

It was the first I'd heard of it.

"When?" asked Maryam. "And why?"

"Yeah, we've never been there!" I said.

"Exactly why we need to go," said Mom.

Dad just chuckled at our confusion before explaining that a close cousin was getting married, so we had to go for the wedding.

Mom and Dad usually daydreamed about taking us on vacations to places that other people talk about. Like Rome to see the Colosseum, or Turkey to see the turquoise waters, or China to see the Great Wall. But Pakistan? For a wedding?!

"Nobody in my class ever talks about vacations in Pakistan," I moaned.

"That's because nobody in your class is *from* Pakistan, silly!" said Maryam.

"I'm not from Pakistan, either," I said. "I'm from England."

"But your grandparents are from Pakistan," said Dad.

"You know you're of Pakistani heritage, darling, as well as being British. It'll be nice for you to learn more about Pakistan," Mom added.

"I'm sure it will be very interesting, Omar," Mrs. Rogers reassured me.

"But what about school?"

"We've asked your schools for some time off because it's a big family event."

Just then, Esa let off the most stinky fart in the universe right at the dinner table.

Maryam, who was sitting next to him, suffered the most. "Oh, Esa!!"

The hilarious thing about Maryam is that if she smells something really stinky, she starts to gag. And that definitely happens for super sure if she is eating when she smells it. I knew it was coming . . .

"BLAAAAAGGGHH!"

Poor Maryam paused and tried to recover

herself. She held her hand to her chest and

closed her eyes.

"BLAAAAA BLAAAAA GGGHH! GGGHH!"

She stood up, put her hand over her mouth

and said, "This is what cabbages would

BLAAAAAGGGHH!

smell like BLAAAAA GGGHH!

if they were

BLAAAAAGGGHH!

evil."

Mom stood up and rubbed her back,

which I didn't think would help at all, so I

shouted out, "Imagine peanut butter cups!"

Those are Maryam's favorite.

"BLAAAAGGGHH!

BLAAAAAGGGHH...

Don't talk about food!" Maryam said, running

out of the room.

Esa was giggling uncontrollably. Probably

feeling pleased that he was able to make such a

show of his bossy big sister.

Mrs. Rogers looked stunned. I guess she still

wasn't used to all the funny things that happen

in our house.

I liked them, and for a few minutes, it made

me forget about Mrs. H.

CHAPTER 11

My friends came over on Saturday
afternoon after I came back from the mosque
with my family. Our first task was to make the
missing posters. They were fun to make. We
had a photo of Mrs. Hutchinson, which Daniel
had snapped from the wall near the office the
day before.

It had been extremely hard, because of Mrs.
Crankshaw making Daniel so nervous.

"What if she's put cameras all over the
school?" Daniel had whispered as we made our

way into the classroom. "Then she can see us from every angle!"

I imagined her as a fruit fly, with lots of eyes all over the place, looking at all the desks at once. Somehow, it suited her to be a fruit fly.

"Don't worry—teachers aren't allowed to record kids, remember?" I had reassured him.

He had his phone in his bag, which is the ONLY place phones are supposed to be if they have to come to school with a kid. Under no circumstances are kids allowed to turn them on or have them in their pocket. While the lesson was happening, I kept glancing at Daniel to see when he was going to put our plan into action. I had never seen him sweat so much as he attempted to fish the phone out of his bag and into his pocket without Mrs. Crankshaw seeing.

What happened next was the exact opposite of how we wanted it to go. It was as if Daniel was trying so hard not to be seen and heard that he accidentally tripled how much he was being seen and heard.

When he was leaning under his desk to take his phone out, he managed to topple his chair all the way forward and go nose-first into the floor, causing a

LOUD CRASHING NOISE

all around him.

I watched from between my fingers as Mrs.
Crankshaw walked menacingly toward him.
Yikes! What if he'd had the phone in his hand
before he fell? She'd see it!

I looked at my poor friend lying in a tangled
heap on the floor. My head was spinning.
Charlie was freaking out across from me.

He was frozen in his chair, **like a deer in headlights**. Everything went into slow motion as I desperately tried to think of what to do . . .

Mrs. Crankshaw's noisy pointy heels were the loudest sound in the room. She was taking long, determined strides toward Daniel. Probably plotting the most severe punishment she could as she went.

What would make her stop? What was an even louder sound?

Yes! I had it. I looked at the huge tin pencil cup sitting on my desk, and quick as lightning, I knocked it to the floor, making the

MOST HORRENDOUS

metal-shattering sound on Earth.

The class winced and put their hands over

their ears. Mrs. Crankshaw stopped walking toward Daniel and spun around to walk toward the atrocity in the opposite direction. In the meantime, about a hundred pencils and markers rolled in all directions on the floor. Some of them must have rolled right under Mrs. Crankshaw's pointy shoe, because suddenly, she stopped walking and **looked like she was trying to balance on ICE,** flapping her arms in the air for support, like some sort of chicken dance. The chicken dance didn't help, though—**she fell,** right on her back, just like they do in cartoons.

The whole class gasped.

I think not so much because they felt bad

for her, but more out of fear of what she would do next.

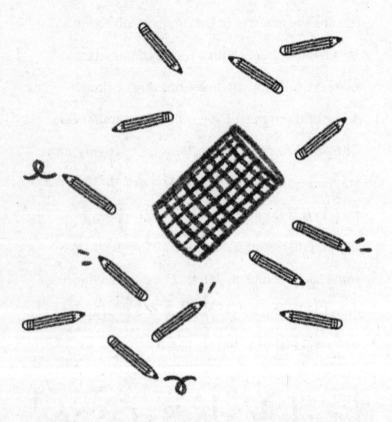

Luckily, she was OK, and managed to sit up, with an embarrassed and extremely angry expression on her face.

I felt really guilty, but I had only meant to create a distraction. Not to make anyone fall over. I went to help her up, giving her my arm to hold on to, like I do with Mrs. Rogers sometimes.

Of course, Daniel quickly took the chance to grab his phone.

"Mrs. Crankshaw, can I go to the bathroom, please?" he said very carefully. "*My nose is bleeding.*"

"Yes, yes," she said, waving him away.

The rest was easy, because the wall with the pictures was around the corner from the office door, so nobody saw Daniel strolling up and taking a picture.

Mrs. Crankshaw made the whole class stay in for break and sharpen every pencil in the room. My hand hurt by the end, and Ellie said she wasn't going to talk to me for a week, but at least we had our picture.

o o o

We decided to put Mrs. H's photo into a Word document. We wanted to type everything out so the posters would be all professional-looking and people would take them seriously.

But it wasn't easy deciding what to put on them.

"Should we write, 'Have you seen any UFOs or strange alien activity?'" suggested Charlie.

"No, that will make us look bonkers!" said Daniel.

"ALiENS DON'T EXIST."

"But other people might have seen that weird alien in disguise doing things around the house," I said.

"You mean the cat," said Daniel. "Maybe Mrs. H shaved it because it had fleas or something."

I decided there was no point in getting upset about Daniel not believing me. There was bound to be some more evidence soon, and then he'd come around.

We had to think about each word because we couldn't put too many words on it— otherwise the text wouldn't be big enough to read from far away. And, well, have you ever tried to say something complicated in just a few words? IT'S HARD!

After a lot of deleting and rewriting and hair pulling,* we finally decided what the poster would say.

"How can people contact us? Should we put a phone number on there, or is that too dangerous?" I asked.

"Too dangerous!" said Charlie and Daniel at the same time.

"Email address, then."

We made up an email address specially for the mission: searchformrsh@dot.com. Pretty cool, right?

---

* I just want to point out that we didn't pull *each other's* hair. We just sort of pulled our own. I've seen my dad do it before when he is typing reports on his computer. It seems to help him—like it actually gives him answers. It made me imagine that maybe Allah has built something special into the hair follicles and when you pull them a little bit, tiny invisible fairies are released that whisper the answers into your ears. It did seem to help us . . . maybe.

Anyway, this is what our poster looked like:

MISSING TEACHER

HAVE YOU SEEN THIS NICE LADY?
If you have information, please email
searchformrsh@dot.com

Next, we borrowed Mom's phone and called Lancelot Macintosh. We had to give Mom a gazillion reasons for being allowed to do that, and make a trillion promises about what we would or would not say.

"Don't ask him if you can have a ride in his Ferrari. And DON'T ask him if he has a butler, and **DEFINITELY** don't tell him aliens took his niece!" she said before she finally asked Siri to call him and stood watching over us.

"Put him on speaker!" said Charlie.

I did.

"Hello?"

"Hello, Lancelot Macintosh!" all three of us said.

"Ah, well, if it isn't the full-name brigade! How are you?" He chuckled.

"Good, thank you," I said.

Mom was whispering to me to ask how he was. She's always teaching me how to be polite.

"How are you?" I asked.

"Ah, fantastic. I'm perfectly fantastic, thanks for asking!"

Mom looked proud.

"We were wondering . . . if you knew anything about, er . . . Mrs. Hutchinson. She's not our teacher anymore and we don't know where she is."

"Oh dear . . . right . . . well. I, ahem . . ." Lancelot Macintosh cleared his throat. "I'm afraid I'm not quite sure I'm at liberty to say . . . erm . . . haha . . ." He laughed awkwardly. "Yes, I don't think I'm supposed to say, actually. Sorry."

"Oh . . ." I said, thinking about how strangely he was behaving.

What wasn't he allowed to say?

Then, as an afterthought, and almost as if he had decided this was what he should have said to us right from the beginning, which made it sound even more secretive, he said, "I haven't heard from that young madam in a while, anyway, ahem."

"Oh . . ."

"I'll try giving her a call and let you know if I hear anything. I'm sure she's fine, though, not to worry!"

I imagined him twiddling his long mustache as he said this, the way he always does.

I hung up the phone.

"Well, that was weird, wasn't it?!" said Daniel.

"Super weird!" I said.

"Soooo weird!" Charlie said.

"It's not weird. It sounded like he just couldn't say. And you know he doesn't *have* to tell you personal things about Mrs. Hutchinson, don't you?" Mom interrupted.

I sighed and gave the phone back to her, saying, "Yessss, Mom." And then I saw her frowning and quickly added, "Thanks for letting us call him."

Mom said, "You should start practicing some words in Urdu for our trip to Pakistan. Do you know how to say 'thank you' in Urdu? Try to remember. You used to say it when you were little. You were so good at repeating the phrases we taught you."

"Erm, no, I don't remember . . ."

"It's Shukriya," she said. Then she repeated it more slowly. "Shook-ree-yah."

"Shukriya," I said. But as soon as she walked out of the room, we went back to wondering what Lancelot Macintosh wasn't allowed to say.

"What do you think he's not telling us?" I asked my friends.

Charlie clapped his face in his hands and gasped with shocked eyebrows. "Do you think he knows who took her?"

"No way!" I said immediately. "That would make him a bad guy, and he's not a bad guy."

"Yeah," Daniel agreed. "It's not that. But maybe he's not telling us about some surprise she's planning for us?"

"Yeah, he's not a bad guy. Sorry. I'm just so worried," said Charlie.

He didn't need to tell me that, because his eyebrows were telling me. Look!

"Don't worry, Charlie. We'll keep trying," I said.

I hoped we'd find her before I went to Pakistan.

We had to.

CHAPTER 12

After calling Lancelot Macintosh, we went out
on our bikes again. I'd had to plead with Mom
and Dad to be allowed to do this. After I had
admitted going beyond the perimeter, they
were feeling

VeRY aNXiouS

about me going out again.

I thought about promising that I wouldn't
do that anymore, but I knew that we needed to,
to keep investigating. I couldn't lie to them.

I shouldn't. I wouldn't. Even though it was really tempting.

Then I remembered that the perimeter rules were only for when I wasn't with Maryam or an adult. So even though it was super annoying and the worst change of plans in the history of the universe, I managed to let out these words in the smallest voice possible, half hoping nobody would hear them:

"What if Maryam went with us?"

"Yes, that would work!" said Mom.

They summoned Maryam to come out of her room, and like some mystical Rumpelstiltskin kind of creature, she emerged on the third callout of her name, still staring at her phone as she walked down the stairs.

"What? No! No way!" she said when Mom explained that she had to babysit my bike ride so we wouldn't be stuck inside for the afternoon.

"Sweetie, we are giving you a big responsibility. You will be in charge. We need you to help us," said Mom, while Dad's eyebrows were telling me he was getting ready to have to use harsher tones.

Anyway, I don't know if it was the thought of being in charge (probably, knowing Maryam), or if it was the sweet way Mom had asked, but Maryam switched her attitude super fast and agreed to go.

"OK, I'll do it!"

PHEW! The mission would go on! Even if it did mean we had to put up with Maryam for the afternoon.

"Get into mission mode!"

I said as all four of us cycled down the
street.

"GUYS! We should think of a code name for
the mission," said Daniel excitedly.

"Like what?" said Charlie with his curious
eyebrows.

"Like Operation Mrs. H."

"That's cool," I said. "But we should be more
secrety," I added, winking at Charlie.

Charlie grinned happily. "Yes, more secrety,
for sure . . . like

Operation Moon Dust

—you know, because it could be an alien
kidnapping!"

"Oh, that's awesome. I love it!" I said, beaming because Charlie was on board with my idea.

"Hmmm," said Daniel. "I'll go along with it, because I like moondust."

"You guys are such geeks," said Maryam, rolling her eyes. "None of you have ever even seen moondust, and there are definitely no aliens on the moon."

"So what?!" I said. "And anyway, yes we have."

"No you haven't," she said.

"Yes we have!" we all said together.

And we went in circles of "no you haven't" and "yes we have" the whole way to our first stop, because we were all too stubborn to give up.

The first stop was the corner store near Mrs. Hutchinson's house.

"People who come here might know something, so let's see if they will let us put a poster up," I said, leaning my bike against the shop window.

A bell rang as we opened the door and walked in.

"Good afternoon," said the man behind the counter. But he said it exactly like it *wasn't* a good afternoon and he hadn't even seen who had come in. We could have been three inside-out cat-aliens and he would be none the wiser.

I walked toward him. He looked startled. I guess he was probably expecting us to wander around forever choosing which candy to spend our money on.

"Sorry," I said. "It's just that my friends and I have a question." I pulled out one of the missing posters from my backpack.

Daniel pushed forward before I had the chance to say anything, excitedly pointing at the poster. "Can we put this up?"

The man looked as if Daniel had asked him if he had seen a walking snake or something.

"No!" he said without even looking at it.

But then Charlie said, "Please? It's for our teacher who is missing." And he smiled his toothy smile.

The shopkeeper finally glanced at the poster and said, "Fine. But you have to buy something."

The three of us looked at each other, silently

asking the question *Got any money?* None of us did, so this seemed like a big flop.

Suddenly, Maryam popped up behind us and said, "I've got some." She pulled out a little yellow coin purse from her jacket, and to our serious surprise, she bought candy for each of

us. Then she took the poster from my hand and

said to the man, in her bossy voice,

"Now please put this up for us."

WOW.

We all made our way excitedly to the exit.

"Thanks, Maryam!" I said.

"Yeah, that was actually really cool of you,"

said Charlie.

And Daniel gave her a spud, which my mom

thinks is a potato, but it's not. It's a fist bump.

"Well, I do want to find out where Mrs.

Hutchinson is, too," she said. "It's kind of

exciting, like one of those murder-mystery

books I read."

Daniel was walking backward through the shop door, because he had spun around for the spud. As he stepped out onto the street, he fell right onto Ellie from our class.

Ellie squealed as if she had just been covered in zombie snot.

"ARGH! Get off me!"

Sarah was with her. "What are you all doing here, anyway?" she said, still on her scooter.

"None of your business!" said Daniel, picking himself up and helping Ellie off the sidewalk.

"We're just buying candy," I said, holding mine up.

Charlie and Daniel both flashed theirs, too, with big grins.

"But this isn't YOUR local shop—" said Ellie.

"Whatever," Daniel interrupted. *"Byeeee!"*
We grabbed our bikes and sped off before
they got any nosier.

"I think she heard what Maryam said about
finding out where Mrs. H is," said Daniel.

"She must have. We were talking really
loudly," said Charlie.

Hmmm, I thought. We
didn't want people at
school knowing what we
were up to. Because if they
told the teachers, they'd either think
we were silly, just like my parents
did, or if they were really in on her
disappearance, then we'd be in
danger.

I had no idea it was also their
local shop. I hoped the

grumpy shopkeeper would wait until they left to put our poster up.

"Let's put the rest of these up on lampposts and trees around the area," I said.

We had brought lots of sticky tape with us. It was quite fun— Operation Moondust! It finally felt like we were doing something to help that could actually work. Someone had to know something, and they would email us soon. I was sure.

We tried to cover lots of roads in the

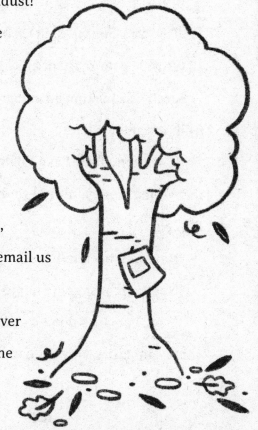

area. When we were making our way to the third road, we heard a scream behind us. It was Ellie and Sarah. Ellie had fallen off her scooter again.

"Have they been following us?!" I said,

PANICKING.

"They're so nosy!" said Charlie.

We rode over to them quickly.

Sarah was picking an embarrassed Ellie up from the sidewalk for a second time.

"It's not my fault I can't balance. I'm still recovering from you!" she said, pointing at Daniel.

"Have you been following us?" I asked.

"No! We're just going home," said Sarah.

"Yeah, you guys don't own the roads, do you?" said Ellie, with her hands on her hips.

"Why are you acting so strange? What exactly are you up to?" said Sarah.

I tried to read her eyebrows, but I couldn't. Did she already know? Had they seen the posters? Or were they question-mark eyebrows? She wouldn't keep them still. She was moving her eyebrows up and down and then one up and one down. It was driving me crazy!

Ellie was staring at us, waiting for an answer, which she wasn't going to get.

"Stop being so nosy and get on with your own business,"

said Maryam.

"Is your knee OK, Ellie?" asked Charlie, blushing. "Did you hurt yourself when you fell down?"

Charlie is always super nice to everyone; it's why we became best friends in the first place. But I suddenly realized we had to get him away before he spilled the beans. If Ellie started sniffling about her sore knee, he would definitely tell her whatever she asked!

"Come on, guys, let's go!" I said, and we pedaled home again. It was time to wrap up Operation Moondust for the day.

CHAPTER 13

For a couple of weeks, we didn't really know what else we could do for Operation Moondust. I had filled Mrs. Rogers in, and she said we had done *great work* but now we just had to wait and see what happened. I didn't tell her about the alien clues, though, just about our posters and Daniel's close encounter with getting caught with his phone in his hand in class.

Until somebody reached out to us with another clue, we had no choice but to carry on our boring lessons with

MrS. CraNky For Sure.

That was the new name everyone in the class

was using for her. Even Sarah, who had been

compared to an angel by more than one of

the teachers at school, had started

calling her by her new name

on the playground (away

from Mrs. C's pointy ears).

I tried to butter up Mrs.

Crankshaw so she'd be nicer

to us all by giving her a scone

that Mrs. Rogers had made. Mrs. Rogers had

winked at me when she brought them over,

saying, "These scones have been known to turn

hearts. Try offering one to your new teacher.

You never know, she might be transformed."

POINTY
EAR

"Wow, thank you!" I had said hopefully.

Esa said, "Shukriya," because he was practicing his Urdu words. Of course, Mom was super impressed with that.

But Mrs. Crankshaw was not impressed at *all* with the scone. She said, "You know you shouldn't bring people food, because you don't know what food allergies they might have!"

"Oh . . . sorry," I said with a lump in my throat.

Charlie had to give me a hug to make me feel better after that. And my stomach wouldn't stop feeling weird all through Language Arts. I felt like I was going to throw up my morning porridge. I have done that before, and it's not very pretty. Porridge isn't the prettiest food in the first place, and after having been in a stomach, it doesn't get any better looking!

Remembering the time I vomited porridge
made me feel even worse, so I stood up quickly
and asked if I could go to the bathroom.

I must have looked kind of green, because Mrs. Crankshaw said yes immediately, and she looked scared when she said it.

When I left the classroom, I felt better straightaway. As if it was the toxic rays from Mrs. C in there that were making me sick. Then a voice popped into my head out of nowhere. And it sounded a lot like Maryam.

"Somebody knows..."

it said.

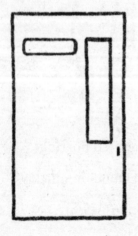

And just like that, my feet turned me toward the staff room, with my heart thumping.

There were no teachers going in and out of the staff room. The hallway was abandoned. But I could hear voices inside. I looked around quickly to make sure no one was coming and put my ear to the door. I had to work hard to make out the words:

"More grading! I wish *mumble* *mumble* long break instead!" said one voice.

"*mumble* *mumble* Hazel?" replied a second voice.

My ears perked up even more, because Hazel is Mrs. Hutchinson's name!

"Ha! Not like she had a choice *mumble* *mumble* She was throwing up left, right and *mumble* *mumble* take her in for tons of tests."

"Just imagine, *mumble* *mumble* living inside you *mumble* *mumble* all that chaos!"

Something living inside her?

"Haha, *mumble* *mumble*
I guess she'll be that way until it comes out
mumble *mumble*"

"Will you visit *mumble* *mumble*?"

"Gosh no, I'm not *mumble* *mumble*
person, they're so weird looking at *mumble*
not even human *mumble**mumble*,
haha."

What I was hearing seemed to confirm everything I had seen and imagined! I quickly walked away with my head in my hands, trying to make sense of it all.

Until it comes out? Something inside her? Making her throw up? Weird looking? Not even human? They took her for tests?

It all fell into place. Of course!

It HAD TO BE aliens!

But it was worse than we had thought: Mrs. Hutchinson had swallowed an alien, so the aliens had taken her away to poke at her until it came out! I couldn't believe our teachers were secretly cooperating with a bunch of aliens—or maybe even *were* aliens themselves!

It was just AWFUL.

When I got back into the classroom, I didn't care about getting in trouble with Mrs. Crankshaw anymore. I couldn't do any work and just stared at my books until recess, when I could talk to my friends.

Mrs. Hutchinson had been taken by aliens! I knew it sounded out of this world, but I was absolutely convinced.

We found a quiet spot, and I spilled everything I'd heard. Charlie was in shock and just opened and closed his mouth loads of times. Daniel said, "But aliens don't exist...?"

It was the same sentence he had been saying ever since we saw the clues at Mrs. Hutchinson's, but now he said it as a question, as if he wasn't sure what to believe anymore.

"Think about it. Mrs. Hutchinson herself said that aliens are out there and they might be watching us!" I said.

"Yeah, and scientists wouldn't be bothering to look for aliens in outer space if they didn't think they existed," added Charlie, recovering from his fish impression.

"Come to think of it, I did see her rubbing her tummy one day . . ." said Daniel. "But how could she have swallowed an alien? Like, why would she?"

"Maybe they're so tiny you can't even see them, and they had come to spy on her for teaching us that alien lesson," I said.

"So she ate it by accident?" said Charlie.

"Yes, *or* she ate it on purpose, to save us, because the aliens were threatening to hurt her class?" I said.

"Wow, she's so brave!" said Charlie.

"But this is CRAZY!" said Daniel, unable to accept it just yet. "There has to be another explanation."

"Sometimes, Daniel, the craziest explanations are the correct ones! Dad told me that happens a lot in science."

"So what are we going to do now?" said Charlie.

We decided it was best to try to speak to some space scientists and do some research on Google on extra-terrestrial visitors to Earth to start with.

Operation Moondust really was going to outer space!

CHAPTER 14

Over the next few days, we spent lunchtimes in the school library, researching everything we could about aliens, mostly for Daniel, who still wasn't convinced that Mrs. Hutchinson had been sucked up into space by them. And man, did we find some weird stuff that absolutely confirmed that aliens were out there and were even found on Earth. Well, the online articles didn't *actually* call them aliens (they called them "organisms"), but they said that these weird tiny squiggly things proved

there was life on other planets. One writer

said the organisms look like dragons, but they

obviously have no idea what dragons look like.

They should see my H_2O—

that's what

a dragon

looks like!

There was a whole universe of stuff to read
on Google. We didn't understand a lot of the
words, and I wished we could ask my parents
to explain them. They'd know about things like
what on earth the Copernican
principle is, but then they'd

know we were still convinced that aliens had abducted our teacher.

Mrs. Hutchinson always said that when we do research, we should look at "sources we can trust," which basically means, if it is written by a famous organization that is known for being right about things, we can usually believe them. But if it's a blog written by people like Maryam and her friends, we should be careful. **WELL!** We found a CNN article, by a NASA chief scientist, saying that they were definitely about to find life on other planets in the coming years. That's two sources we could trust.

"Do you see, Daniel?" said Charlie excitedly. "Do you belieeeeeeeve?" And he spun Daniel's whirly chair around to look him in the eyes for extra-dramatic effect.

Just then, Ellie and Sarah walked into the library with extra-nosy expressions painted all over their faces.

"Does he believe what?" pressed Ellie.

They tried to look at our computer screen, but I quickly closed the window AND stood in front of it, just in case.

Charlie frantically gathered the few books on space that we had found on the shelves and sat on them.

We wouldn't share our secret, no matter how much they bugged us to, so they went to sit down and pretended to read some books on history. Sarah and Ellie hated history lessons,

So we KNEW
they were
just spying.

We had to leave then, but we felt super proud of ourselves for doing all that research, and even being able to convince Daniel (sort of). The next time we were able to get into the library, we found an email contact for NASA and sent them all the details from our searchformrsh@dot.com address. Perhaps they would send out a special search mission in space for her? After all, it was their job, wasn't it? We kept a close eye on our inbox, but they didn't reply to us, no matter how much we checked.

While we waited for something to happen, we tried to get on with our lives as if everything was normal. Even though Maryam had been nice about helping us put the missing posters up, we didn't share our alien abduction idea with her, because she would

DEFiNiTELY

LAUGH AT US

and tell all her friends, who would also join in with the laughing. I had to keep it to myself at home, which was HARD.

Maybe because of all the keeping it to myself inside my head, I saw aliens everywhere. Instead of seeing regular old fruit flies, I would see tiny flying aliens and imagine them growing into something much bigger and slimier when they landed on a surface. And instead of seeing Esa's green snot as regular green snot, I would see it as alien slime.

One day, when we were in a mall and I was

desperate for the bathroom, I could have sworn I saw an alien peek his head out of one of the toilets, to see if anyone was around.

CHAPTER 15

At home, things were very busy as Mom and Dad prepared for our trip to Pakistan.

My friends were

super jealous

about me being allowed to take time off school and go on vacation while they had to have boring lessons with Mrs. CrankyForSure.

"We will probably literally die of boredom without you, Omar," said Charlie. "Can you clone yourself and leave one of you here?"

"Yeah, do that! You're good at science, you can figure it out," Daniel added.

I giggled, imagining myself as a clone.

Would my clone have all of my memories? Would he be good at science, too?

"What's Pakistan like, anyway?" Charlie asked.

"I have NO CLUE. The only thing I've heard was from my cousin, who said the pizza is yuck," I said.

I soon found out another thing about the food in Pakistan, because one Tuesday, Dad came home with three bags full of chocolate.

WHAAAAAT?

Three bags of my favorite food?

Obviously, Esa, Maryam and I pounced on him right away, attempting to wrestle him to the ground to steal all the bags.

Dad laughed and then roared and said, "Hulk angry," pretending to be angry, which we knew he wasn't.

Then he said, "Actually . . . Hulk hungry! What's for dinner, O mother of mischievous children?"

Mom laughed and said that we were *his* children when we were mischievous, and we were only hers when we were little angels like she is.

"I want chocolate for dinner," said Esa.

"Well, these chocolates are for all the different families we will visit in Pakistan. The chocolate they get out there is nowhere as good as this stuff," said Dad.

"Pleeeeease . . . I will say shukriya?" said Esa, making his puppy eyes.

Everyone laughed at his suggestion. Usually Esa would laugh, too, but for some reason he stood still, thinking. Then he asked very carefully, "Mom? How do you laugh in Urdu?"

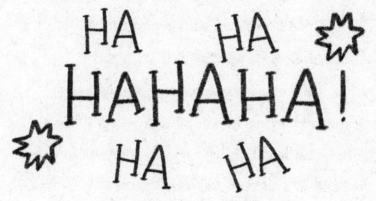

That was the best thing Esa had said in a while.

In the end, Dad allowed us to have some of the chocolate if we could prove he had a brain. He likes to play games with us like that.

"You do have one, obviously!" said Maryam. "Otherwise, how could you be a scientist?"

"That's not proof. Mrs. Rogers isn't a scientist; does that mean she doesn't have a brain?" teased Dad.

"You have one because you're talking and walking and things!" I said.

"Good!" said Dad, winking my way. "I'd definitely need a brain for that."

"OK, you have one because you're human, and all humans have brains. We know that because scientists have looked at lots of human bodies," said Maryam, trying harder.

"Excellent!" said Dad, and he rewarded us with a bar each.

Maryam doesn't like science like the rest of our family. She's always grumpy on

Science Sundays,

which is when we do fun science experiments in the kitchen. And one day recently when Mom was tutoring Maryam on science, she seemed super bored, and then she suddenly burst out crying. It was a painful crying, like something really, really bad had happened.

"Maryam, what is it?" asked Mom, jumping to put her arms around her. "Has something happened in school? Tell me."

Maryam continued to cry, like she was being tortured.

"Maryam, sweetie, please tell me. I can't help you if you don't tell me," pleaded Mom.

"YOU'RE TRYING TO MAKE ME GOOD AT SCIENCE!"

Mom looked shocked. "I thought that was nice of me," she said. "Pardon me, young lady, I thought I was helping you!"

Mom tried to be angry when she said that, but she found Maryam's reason for crying very, very funny and she couldn't hold it in for long. She burst out laughing, which made Maryam cry even more.

Mom hugged her and told her that she was already good at science, but if she loved other subjects more, the way she loved art, she could be something creative instead of being a scientist.

It seemed like that made Maryam feel a whole lot better.

CHAPTER 16

With a one-week countdown to our trip, I started to get REALLY excited about having a break from Mrs. Crankshaw. Why? Because she had banned smiling in class! We didn't suspect her of being a supervillain for no reason.

It had happened on a day when we were learning about South America. Obviously, Mrs. Crankshaw had made it boring with her super-boring-making powers. She had asked us to read about it from a textbook and "take notes." Daniel finds that kind of thing impossible, so instead of getting on with it, he busied himself by leaning on the two back legs of his chair and smiling over at Charlie and me.

We had a whole

smile conversation.

Sheesh, this is boring, smiled Daniel.

Super definitely, I smiled back.

Can't wait till lunchtime, smiled Charlie.

Can't wait till summer, smiled Daniel.

But that was his last smile for a bit, because just then, there was a big

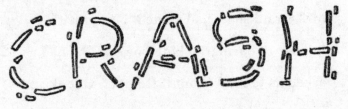

as the two back legs of Daniel's chair gave in, and he went tumbling into the book display behind him. What was it with Daniel always falling off his chair?

"Enough!!!" screamed Mrs. Crankshaw.

"I've been watching you, Daniel Green. All of this happened because of your silly smiling. There will be no more silly smiling. Do you hear that, everyone? There will be no more smiling in this class, ever."

And she stamped her pointy heel on the ground like she was an army general and wrote

on the board.

We were miserable during lunchtime. Why did Mrs. CrankyForSure have to be so mean?

We tried to think of the reasons:

"Maybe she was bitten by a mysterious bug from Mars that makes people grumpy for the rest of their days," I said.

"Maybe she has Grumpy Nut Cornflakes for breakfast every morning," said Charlie.

"Maybe she farts toxic fumes that make her angry and mean when she accidentally breathes them in," said Daniel.

We had a good giggle at that, which cheered us up a little, and we decided to spend some of lunchtime in the school library so we could check the inbox for an email from NASA. Operation Moondust was always on our mind.

I logged in, without much hope, because the last thirty-eight times I had done this, there was no email. But as the page loaded, our eyes fell on an email with the subject line:

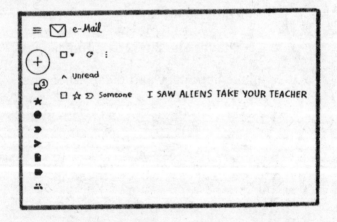

I nearly fell off my chair, and Daniel gave Charlie an excited whack on the back, which

was way too hard and sent him off on a
sputtering coughing fit.

When we all recovered enough, I said, "Let's
open it . . ."

It read:

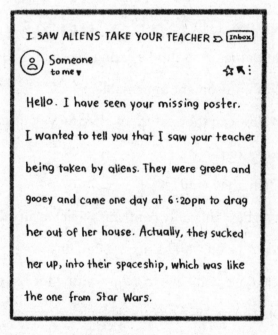

I SAW ALIENS TAKE YOUR TEACHER ⇥ [Inbox]

Someone
to me ▾   ☆ ⇤ ⋮

Hello. I have seen your missing poster.

I wanted to tell you that I saw your teacher

being taken by aliens. They were green and

gooey and came one day at 6:20pm to drag

her out of her house. Actually, they sucked

her up, into their spaceship, which was like

the one from Star Wars.

We were utterly gobsmacked. Even Daniel
didn't say a word for a long time.

"Poor Mrs. Hutchinson," I said eventually.

"I can't believe it," said Charlie with sad eyebrows.

"I will destroy those aliens! And make them eat avocados!" said Daniel, who thinks eating avocados is the worst punishment imaginable.

"How can they eat them after they're dead?" asked Charlie.

"Oh, they will!"

"I guess this only confirms what we already know," I said. "And since we don't have a rocket, we will have to keep waiting for help from the real astronauts. They have to help! Maybe they are, secretly, already?"

Still, the pictures that email had put in our heads were terrible. It made everything more real. And now we had a description of the aliens. Green and gooey. Mrs. H must have been terrified. I imagined what her hair looked like when she was scared. Probably the way they show it in cartoons when someone gets an electric shock. All the curls rigid and standing on end.

CHAPTER 17

We spent the whole rest of the week not

smiling in class. Even during the last lesson on

Friday, which meant a weekend was beginning

and everyone would normally be *super*

happy. During that lesson, though,

it sort of looked like Mrs. Crankshaw might

be smiling. Her mouth was turning up at the

corners ever so slightly, but as if it hurt to do

it. I guessed that she was happy because she

had managed to invent the most miserably

boring lesson possible.

Charlie noticed it first and pointed at me as

we tried to keep our eyes open. "Hey . . . is

Mrs. CrankyForSure *smiling*?"

"No *way* . . ." I whispered.

"Should we ask her if the smile ban has been

lifted?"

That made me laugh. I had just taken a

sip from my water bottle, and it came out of

my nose. OUCH, that kills!

Never, ever laugh with a drink in your mouth.

If I was an alien who had come to Earth for

the first time, and I came to Mrs. Crankshaw's

class, I would think that all teachers were

grumpy and boring. But they're not. I know

that because of Mrs. Hutchinson. She really,

really is

the best.

o o o

We left for Pakistan the next day, from
Heathrow Airport.

Mrs. Rogers waved us off from her front
yard with a tear in her eye.

"We'll be back before you know it, Mrs.
Rogers," said Dad.

"Oh, I disagree. I'm afraid I'll miss you all
too much!"

We gave her hugs and thanked her for
the treats she had baked for us to have on
the way.

"I'll bring you back something Pakistani,"
I said.

"You're the only Pakistani thing I need," she
joked.

I smiled at the thought of her finding the
little notes I had left around her house when

she fell asleep on the sofa the evening before we were leaving.

In her teapot: "I miss you, too, Mrs. Rogers."

Halfway through the book she's reading:

"Here's a joke for you: Why don't aliens eat clowns? Because they taste funny!"

Behind a sofa cushion:

"Will you finally tell me your big secret from when you were younger, when I get back?"

Inside her special gardening shoes:

"Are you surviving without Pakistani food?"

On the plane, we did what we always do. Maryam and I fought for the **window seat,** and Esa and I fought to sit next to Dad. We each had our own backpack full of things to keep us busy, and as a special travel treat, **we had candy!**

Mom made us pack books to read and puzzles to do, because she didn't want us to continuously watch movies for the whole eight-hour flight.

Even with all the stuff to do, the flight was

LOOOOONG.

I felt odd being stuck in one seat for eight hours, with nowhere to go except a smelly bathroom that made a scary noise when you flushed the toilet. I looked out the window

and wondered how much farther up
I would have to go to get to space. I
imagined my dragon, H_2O, picking me
up from the wing of the plane and
flying us both upward,

like a rocket.

Then I thought about the second message we had received from the same person to our MrsH email address. I had seen it just before we'd had to rush to the car that morning, so I hadn't had a chance to tell Daniel or Charlie yet. It said:

I saw her swallow an alien by the way. And I know where she is.

Who was this person? How did they know so much? Was it her neighbor? Or the funny man at the corner store?

We finally started seeing Pakistan from way up high, before we made a smooth landing at Lahore International Airport. That's a big city in Pakistan.

My uncle came to pick us up from the airport. He isn't *really* my *uncle* uncle—he's my dad's older cousin—but in Pakistan we knew to call all the adults in the family **uncle** and **aunty,** and all the kids **cousin.** He had a mustache like Lancelot Macintosh's, and no hair, which made me giggle, because he looked like an **egg with a mustache.**

I kept that to myself, because I knew Mom would absolutely *not* be proud of me for making fun of the way someone looks. Well, it wasn't making fun if I only thought it inside my head and didn't put it into anyone else's head.

On the drive to my uncle's house, I decided **I already loved Pakistan.**

It was different from anyplace I had ever seen. The cars were all beeping and bouncing into whichever lanes they wanted, and every so often, there was a random donkey pulling a cart in the same lane as all the cars and three-wheeled vehicles, called rickshaws, which looked like they were part of a circus act! It was noisy and crowded, but it was

AMAAAAAAZiNG!

CHAPTER 18

The  houses were big in Pakistan.
Well, at least my

uncle's was, and all the others I saw from

the car. There were maids at his house, too,

who cleaned up after us and served us

yummy food,

which was better than my mom's Pakistani

cooking.

I asked Mom if everyone in Pakistan had a

maid, or if my uncle was a billionaire like the

queen or something. She told me that it was

quite common and laughed at the idea that our

family was **$UP£R RICH.**
Can you imagine having a maid at home? I couldn't believe it!

I had twin cousins, called Amber and Ambreen, who always wore matching shalwar kameez, which is the traditional Pakistani outfit of a tunic over soft trousers. **It made it really hard to tell them apart,** which they enjoyed very much.

"You talk so fast," they kept saying in their Pakistani accent. And they would giggle forever when Maryam and I got into a squabble and called each other names like

FROG FACE

and

RHINO NOSE.

My aunty didn't say much, but she always made a point to tell her daughters to stop giggling.

Early in the mornings, **I would hear the strangest calls.**

It sounded like a man's voice, but I couldn't make out what he was saying. It wasn't the call to prayer, which is called **the adhan,** because I knew exactly what that sounded like. I heard it lots when we went on vacation to Turkey once, and I was hearing it in Lahore, too, coming from the mosques. But I needed to know what this other morning call was.

So, one day, the minute I heard it, I ran to the balcony. I saw a man pulling a cart full of fresh vegetables, calling out:

"Aaloooooo layyyyllo,

pYaaaaz layyyyllo,

gaaajar layyyyyyyyllo!"

I asked Amber and Ambreen what he was saying, although I could tell it was something about the vegetables.

"He's saying, 'Get potatoes, get onions, get carrots!'" They both giggled almost at the same time, finding it hilarious that I didn't understand Urdu.

So I said, "Shukriya," for fun. Because it was about the only word I could remember at the time.

After a few days, we went to meet Yusuf, the man who was getting married—the reason I was missing school and had come all the way to a place I had never been to before. He was my mom's aunty's son. **I got very confused** about whether that meant I should call him a cousin, even though he wasn't a kid. But Mom said he could just be

"Uncle," too! Apparently, Mom used to go to Pakistan on vacation a lot before she got busy being an IMPORTANT SCIENTIST and had us kids, so she had been quite close with this part of the family, and it was out of the question for her not to be here to share the joy. Although, I think Mom was just excited to have an excuse to show us the country her parents were from. (In case you're wondering, my grandparents had decided not to come on this trip. My nani said we were all representing them at the wedding, so we had to be on our best behavior.)

Uncle Yusuf was really nice, so I was glad we had come. "This is the groom—Yusuf," Mom said proudly.

"He's not a broom!"

said Esa.

Yusuf laughed and pulled out all sorts of presents for us. He was a giant man, even taller than Dad, but he had a super-gentle voice. Esa looked tiny in front of him, and when Yusuf picked him up, he did it as carefully as if Esa was made of

eggshells.

"What have they been feeding you at Aunty and Uncle's?" He laughed as he popped Esa on his shoulder. "Shrinking powder? This little man looks about the same size as my head!"

After meeting him, I was looking forward to going to his big wedding. I wanted to see what the bride was like.

I hoped she'd be kind, like him.

CHAPTER 19

One evening, when were all sitting around
at my uncle and aunty's house, my aunty
announced that the special wedding outfits
she had arranged to be made for us had finally
arrived.

They were wrapped in colorful cotton
sheets, which she excitedly opened up, one
by one.

Ouch, the shirt for me looked
really uncomfortable, with a rock-hard collar.

They were the same type of thing that my cousins wear every day, except extra fancy.

Maryam liked hers a lot, probably because it looked like a princess dress, with sparkly patterns and beads. She even got some gold shoes to go with it.

GOLD! SUPER YUCK!

Of course, I was forced to try mine on, so I took it to the twins' room, which was closest. I put it on the bed and wasted some time before having to put it on by snooping around a bit. They were always laughing at me for not knowing how to speak Urdu—maybe I would find something to tease them about . . .

There wasn't much around. Only some books

and board games. But just when I was about to give up on finding anything interesting, my foot tapped something hard. I looked down.

FLYING FiSH EGGS!

It was a telescope! What were Amber and Ambreen doing with a telescope?

I threw my wedding outfit on in a millisecond (it didn't actually look too bad) so I could go and ask them about it.

"To look into outer space, of course," said Amber.

WOW!

Who knew they would be so cool!

I liked them ten times*

more, right on the spot.

Maryam and I begged them to let us try it.

"Pleeeease show us how to look at the planets!" I said, obviously thinking of Mrs. H. It was a long shot, but maybe I would see an alien spaceship or something. Maybe there would be more clues that would help our search.

As it turned out, Amber and Ambreen knew lots about space. They were huge space geeks.

They let us take turns, excitedly telling us what to look for.

"I've been on another planet," said Esa.

"No you haven't, Esa," I told him.

"Yes I did go!" Esa protested.

"No," said Maryam. "Don't lie."

"I did! When I wasn't listening, Dad said, 'He's on another planet.' So there!"

Amber and Ambreen giggled and pulled Esa's cheek.

"You're sooooo cute," they said.

It was my turn to look. I took hold of the telescope carefully.

"Have you ever seen a spaceship or an alien?" I asked, trying to be casual.

Maryam said, "Of course they haven't, pineapple prickles! Because aliens don't exist."

"Actually, they might,"

said Amber.

"They probably do," said Ambreen.

Maryam rolled her eyes.

"Wow . . . did you see something?" I asked, wide-eyed.

"Yes, we see strange things all the time, but we don't know what they are."

"Do you think they ever come down to Earth?" I paused. "And . . . er . . . take stuff?"

At that, Maryam exploded with laughter and let herself fall to the floor to roll around holding her belly, to show just how funny it was.

"OMAR! You think they took Mrs. Hutchinson, don't you?" she teased.

"No!" I lied. "Of course not!"

But Maryam fanned the air, pretending she couldn't even breathe with how hilarious it was, and then walked out of the room.

"Who's Mrs. Hutchinson?" asked Amber.

"Never mind . . ." I whispered with a lump in my throat. And I quickly walked away before they noticed how sad I was.

CHAPTER 20

I liked Yusuf so much that I didn't mind putting on the uncomfortable fancy wedding clothes when it was time. When I looked in the mirror,

I looked like a different kid!

Like my own Pakistani twin.

Amber and Ambreen were wearing matching outfits. Maryam had put on her princess clothes and looked very pleased with herself. She was trying to take selfies on her phone to show her friends.

The house was busy with people running around looking for their shoes or putting on lipstick. My dad was standing at the door shouting about getting into the car already, which my uncle found hilarious.

"Don't worry, everybody will be late. **Nobody goes On time,**" he said, chilling out on the sofa.

"What? Uncle? Are you even dressed?" asked Dad.

"No, no, the ladies will take too long. I will get dressed in a minute." He chuckled.

This was very difficult for Dad, who thinks it's the end of the world to be late to anything. So being told he had to be late on purpose was pretty much the same as being told he had to eat through his nose! He checked his watch longingly and sat down uncomfortably in his outfit.

We finally piled into the car. When we arrived, we saw Uncle was totally right: EVERYONE was late.

Now, I've been to Pakistani weddings in London before, but this was something different. It was crazy!

Good crazy, _not_ WILD CRAZY.

It was outdoors, but in a

BIG MARQUEE,

which is just a fancy word for a tent that is the size of a house. It was decorated with lights—so many of them, on the inside and outside! There were hundreds and hundreds of people there. In a way, it was like a game, because there were "sides." We were on the groom's side, which meant we had to make a *Grand Entrance* with him.

You're not going to believe this, but Yusuf made his entrance on a horse. A dressed-up horse! And the horse looked just big enough to take his weight, but only just. And there were other horses that were dancing. A few men were playing the biggest drums I have ever seen, which they hung around their necks. The sound was

HUGE.

And it was a good tune. It made me want to

dance walk, instead of normal walk, my way into the marquee.

The people on the bride's side were already inside, and they threw lots of flower petals on

us as we walked in. Together with the fancy

clothes everyone was wearing, it was a

BIG EXPLOSION OF COLORS.

Esa was loving it and Maryam was trying to love it, but she was also busy complaining about how **itchy** her princess dress turned out to be. Amber and Ambreen looked like they weren't seeing anything special, probably because they see these kinds of big Pakistani weddings all the time.

Then the bride came in. Maryam's princess clothes were nothing compared to hers. She was wearing a dark red dress that was so long, she couldn't actually walk unless someone was lifting it for her a bit.

It looked **HEAVY**, too, with **MILLIONS** of GEMS and BEADS.

Yusuf and his bride, Aisha, sat together, and then a man in a hat and a beard came to talk to them.

"That's the imam," Mom explained. **"He's going to *marry* them now."**

A lot of people were still chatting away, which I thought was crazy. "They're missing it!" I said.

It was over in just a couple of minutes. He just asked them to say some words and sign a paper, and that was it! Yusuf was married to Aisha, **and half the people missed it!**

When the food came, I couldn't believe how much there was. There were so many things to eat, I couldn't even try them all. Most of it was too full of chili for me, anyway—which is weird, because I thought **I LOVED** spicy food.

And at the end, when it was time for the bride and groom to go, everyone cried lots and lots like something bad had happened. That was super weird. It was a wedding and weddings are supposed to be happy, right?

"Why are they crying?"

I asked Maryam.

"Probably because their clothes are too uncomfortable," she replied, tugging her itchy dress away from her skin and walking painfully in her golden heels.

"It's sort of like a tradition," explained Dad. "It's the girl's side that is crying, because they are sad that she's leaving their family."

"But she's not, is she? She'll be back and still see them?" I asked.

"Of course," said Dad.

Traditions were funny things sometimes, I guessed.

I imagined Yusuf as a giant alien in disguise that was abducting her and taking her to outer space forever on his dancing horse, which seemed funny for a minute until I remembered that that's exactly what could have happened to Mrs. H.

I gulPed.

CHAPTER 21

Now that the wedding events were over, we
had more free time. I looked through the
telescope every chance I could get. I was glued
to it one evening when we were supposed
to be going out to a restaurant for dinner.
Everyone had been looking for me around
the big house, and I didn't hear them calling,

so Maryam was super mad when she had to come and find me.

"There you are! You're so **obsessed** with that thing," she said.

"Hurry up."

Oh man, just when I was trying to get a mysterious flying object back into focus! I had to drop it and run.

On the way to the restaurant it was really windy. But it wasn't just a regular wind—it was blowing dirt around everywhere, so we couldn't open the car windows. Apparently, that kind of wind happens all the time in Lahore.

When we got to the restaurant parking lot, it was filled with fancy cars. A man came to knock on the windows of the car, putting his hand out. His clothes were dirty and torn and he didn't have any shoes on. My uncle tried to shoo him away.

"Mom, what's that man saying?" I asked.

"Oh, Sweetie, he's a poor man. He's asking for money."

Dad pulled out a couple of notes of Pakistani currency and handed them to him. The man started saying lots of things in Urdu.

"Now what's he saying?" I asked.

"He's praying for goodness and blessings for Dad," said Mom.

I felt so sad for the poor old man. He didn't have any money, and all the people in the fancy cars obviously had lots.

Just then, many more poor people started coming up to Dad, making it impossible for

him to get out of the car. My uncle shooed
them away, muttering angry Urdu words.

I wished I had Lots of my own money to give them.

"Can we invite them to dinner?" I asked as
we were walking into the restaurant.

"Of course we can't, gerbil brains," said
Maryam.

I paused and turned around just to have one
more look at them. But when I did, I almost fell
to the ground because of what I saw . . .

It was Mrs. Hutchinson !!!

She was getting into a black Toyota and her
belly was

BIG.

I couldn't believe my eyes. I blinked a few
times, just to make sure. **It WAS her.**
Every bit of curly hair and her smile and A BIG
BELLY! We had been looking for her for ages,
and suddenly she was right before my eyes,
driving away in a car.

My legs threatened not to hold me up
anymore, but fast as I could, I rushed in and
found my parents. I told them I needed to speak
to my friends right away. I was a **TOTAL**
mess.

"Just a minute. What is going on?" said Dad.

"Mrs. Hutchinson's on Earth, I mean she's
come back down to Earth, she's here, I just

saw her and her tummy is big, like

THE ALIEN IS STILL IN THERE, She must have

escaped. She MUST have swallowed an alien.

What is she doing HERE? Maybe she landed

in the complete wrong country. Maybe she

was with the FBI. Maybe she IS FBI.

Argggghhghhghgh,"

I sputtered all in one go.

"Wow," said Mom.

My uncle and aunty

were looking at me as if

they had in that

moment decided

that all British kids were completely **bonkers.**

They were looking from me to Mom and Dad

and nodding their heads as if in agreement with their own thoughts.

"Right, take a seat, son," said Dad, and he poured me a glass of water. "Tell me what you're talking about, calmly."

Hmmm, could I? I knew it was unbelievable to them. I felt like I'd already said too much, so I stayed quiet.

"Him and his weird friends think Mrs. Hutchinson was abducted by aliens," teased Maryam.

SHE MADE iT SOUND SO STUPiD.

"Are you still on that?" asked Mom.

"Sort of," I said, even though I one hundred percent was.

"Let's calm down and have some food, darling. You're just hungry and tired," said Mom, and she gave me a hug.

"Well, she could have swallowed an alien . . ." said Dad, causing all the heads to spin around to glare at him.

"Kidding!" he said, having a good chuckle.

"Am I not allowed to have an imagination like my boy's?"

And just like that, everyone settled down and took their plates around the fabulous buffet, collecting all sorts of fancy foods. But I had lost my appetite.

CHAPTER 22

I hated Maryam for making my idea sound stupid in front of Mom and Dad, but she was the only one I could talk to about it all.

I told her that **I HADN'T imagined seeing Mrs. Hutchinson.**

"When I imagine things, I know I'm imagining them, Maryam. I know the difference between seeing something and imagining it . . ."

"I get that," said Maryam.

PHEW! I must have caught the good Maryam. She's a teenager, so sometimes she changes from being good to evil Maryam in minutes.

"Thanks for believing me."

"So you saw her? Who was she with?"

"I don't know. I just saw her getting into a car."

"OK. But you do know that the outer space thing is completely crazy, right?"

"We have lots of proof," I tried.

"You *think* you do," Maryam said.

"Do you think we can go back to that restaurant and look for her again?"

"Probably not. Anyway, it's not as if she would eat there every night. But we can look for her every time we go out."

"OK," I said. At least that was something.

But we needed all the help we could get, so I lifted my hands up to make a dua and asked Allah to help. That had worked in the past, when I was lost with Daniel in central London.

"*Oh, Allah*. I'm really worried about Mrs. Hutchinson. Can you help me find her, please? And can you make her be OK? I don't even mind being wrong about the alien stuff, because that would mean that poor Mrs. H wouldn't have had to go through something so bad. Thank you, Allah. *Ameen.*"

Mom and Dad were calling us just then, because we were going to go shopping and to visit some other relatives. Dad was holding one of the bags of chocolate in his hand.

In the car, he passed over some money for me, and some for Maryam, to spend at the shops.

"I don't know what you'll find, Omar, other than ladies' clothes and jewelry, but enjoy it anyway." He winked.

He was right. There were rows and rows of men selling colorful fabrics for ladies to have their clothes sewn. Apparently, that's the way most people do it in Pakistan instead of buying ready-made clothes. Some ladies sounded like they were arguing with the stall holders. Mom said they were haggling for the price, which is also the normal way to shop.

"So you want to try to give them less money than they're asking for?" I said.

"Basically, yes," said Mom.

"**But that's not fair**. They look poor," I said.

"Well, they know you'll do it, so they ask for much more than it's worth anyway," explained Mom.

I liked how busy it was, and how colorful. Everyone seemed to be enjoying themselves. We stopped at the stall of one man who only had hair around the sides of his head, but he had grown it long on one side and combed it over the top of his head, as some sort of baldness disguise. As Mom haggled with him over the price of fabric, the wind blew and the unfortunate hair flapped upward, revealing the man's NoT-So-SECRET SECRET.

"Seven hundred rupees. Bas," said the man, being firm and serious. But his hair wouldn't sit back down—it was like a flag flapping around at the top of a big, shiny mast.

It was such a funny sight, I wanted to burst out laughing. But I was controlling it the best I could, trying to look anywhere else but his head. It wasn't working. The hilarious hair was all my eyes would look at. I tried not to glance at Maryam, because I knew if I did and she was trying not to laugh as well, I would be able to tell, and then I would lose control.

Mom quickly gave in, handed him the cash and sped away, as Maryam and I slapped our hands over our giggles.

I hadn't forgotten to keep an eye out for Mrs. Hutchinson. I thought I heard her voice for a minute, so I followed it, just a little away from where Mom and Dad were buying bangles for Mrs. Rogers.

But when I got through the crowd of people and arrived at the human with the voice and tapped her shoulder, it wasn't Mrs. H. And I was in BIG TROUBLE for walking off, because I had sent Mom and Dad into a complete panic.

"OMAR! You NEVER walk away from us. NEVER. Especially in a city like LAHORE!" screamed Mom frantically.

"Yeah, that was pretty stupid," said Maryam.

"Were you looking for something to spend your money on?" asked Dad.

"Ermm, yes. I guess," I said.

Mom insisted on holding my hand for a while, even though I'm not a baby like Esa. The shopping took forever, and it got **Super boring**. We found a toy shop, and I stopped to look at some things, but instead, I gave my money to a poor lady on the floor who was rocking her baby.

CHAPTER 23

After shopping, we went to the house of
relatives, who were Dad's uncle's cousin's
grandchildren, or something long like that.
My uncle drove us there. He basically went
everywhere with us, like a bodyguard or
something.

There were a couple of goats outside
their front door. Pakistan has lots of random
animals like that. The relatives were grateful
for the bag of chocolate. They looked as if they
had just been given a bag of diamonds.

They kept asking Esa how old he was and

what his name was and then cooing and
gushing when he got it right.

Maryam whispered in my ear, "He's *three*,
he's not *dumb*. What's so impressive?"

I shrugged and tried to get through the
funny food on my plate, which was way too full
of chili.

When it was time to leave, I was So
Glad. I was looking forward to
doing something more fun than shopping and
visiting people's houses.

Dad asked if he could drive on the way back.

"Are you sure, darling?" Mom asked.

"The traffic here is bonkers."

"Nothing I can't handle," said Dad.

He was right. He wove in and out of the crazy, jumpy cars and tooted his horn for no reason, just like everyone else was doing.

I had my eyes peeled, making sure he didn't hit a donkey or a rickshaw. It was lots of fun. Like some sort of video game where you had to drive along avoiding the obstacles and collecting points. I imagined the red cars were points if Dad overtook them, and the black cars were villains.

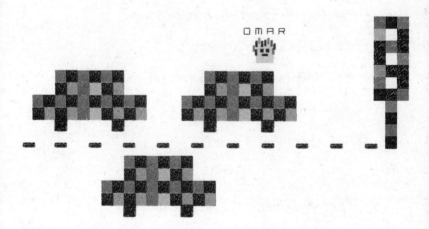

Then, as I was looking at everything on the road, Mrs. Hutchinson's face appeared at the window of the same black Toyota I had seen at the restaurant. Her head was turned my way, but she was looking right past me.

OH MY GOD!

It's Mrs. Hutchinson!" I shouted.

"Not again," said Mom right away.

"Where?" said Maryam.

The Toyota had overtaken us. I could see it slightly up ahead. In a panic, I screamed, "Dad! Follow that black Toyota!"

"Omar! No!" said Mom.

"Are you certain?" asked Dad.

"Yes!" I screamed again.

"Listen to him!" shouted Maryam.

"Don't listen to them, darling!" shouted Mom.

My uncle was making Urdu comments that I didn't understand, but the hand motions seemed to say, "Omar is crazy for sure, and why are you all shouting?"

"I have to help him!" shouted Dad, and he stepped on the accelerator so hard, everyone's heads hit their headrests.

"YESSSSSS, DAD! YOU'RE THE BESSSSST!"

Dad was on the Toyota's tail in seconds, just like I knew he would be, but there was a traffic light coming up and it went red. Dad sped through it anyway.

"What are you doing???!!" yelped Mom.

"Look around—nobody stops at the reds around here," said Dad, jumping lanes and cutting in close in front of a white Audi to get behind the Toyota.

"You're as bonkers as your kids," said Mom, but I could tell she was enjoying the excitement, and she was beginning to smile and trying to hide it.

"Daddy is so fast!" Esa laughed.

The black Toyota took a left. Dad took the left. Then it took a right. Dad took it, too, but he just skimmed a fruit stall on the corner, where someone had piled up a load of apples in a pyramid. They all tumbled down behind us.

"Oh bananas!!!" said Dad, looking in his mirrors. "I have to stop and sort that out."

"NOOOOOOOOO," said Mom, to my utter surprise. "We'll go back and help him later!"

YES! I knew Mom had it in her.

We were on the Toyota's heels again, traveling down a long, narrow road. It was going fast, as if it knew it was being chased.

"Maybe she thinks the aliens are chasing her, or the FBI," I said to Maryam.

Suddenly, the Toyota turned into the gates

of a house. We parked outside. I held my

breath for what felt like ages, waiting for the

moment that would reveal everything. Waiting

for her to step out of the car . . .

CHAPTER 24

We all stared at the black Toyota. The driver stepped out first, then an older man, and eventually the door I had been watching opened slowly, and out stepped my wonderful teacher.

"See! See! It's her!" I said.

PHEW! I didn't look silly in front of my family again. Everyone knew that bouncy, springy hair. It was Mrs. H all right. No doubt about it.

"Let's go," I said, one leg already out of the car door.

"We can't just go and invade their privacy," said Mom, too polite as always.

"Yes, we can," said Dad. "Let's put this thing to bed, eh?"

So we did.

Mrs. Hutchinson was shocked. **"Omar?! What on earth are you doing here?"**

I loved seeing her hair expressing more shock than her words, moving magically right before my eyes.

"What are **YOU** doing here?" I asked.

"Well, I guess I never told you this, but this is my husband," she explained, gesturing to the bewildered-looking man beside her. The driver of the black Toyota. "My husband is Pakistani, like you, Omar. We're here for a visit."

WOW.

We all sat down with a cup of tea and some samosas, and I told Mrs. Hutchinson everything. Right from the start, peeking over at my parents every now and then, because they didn't know the half of it.

A couple of times, Mom wanted to jump in to say she couldn't believe all this was going on, but I saw Dad put a hand on her knee to tell her to keep it in for now.

Mrs. Hutchinson had listened very carefully, sometimes with shock and sometimes with amusement. But she didn't interrupt. She just let me finish.

"And . . . well . . . is that it?" I pointed to the bump that was her tummy. "Is that the alien baby?"

"Well . . ." Mrs. H spoke slowly, as if she was choosing her words carefully. "It is a baby, but it's not an alien. It's my baby. I'm having a baby, Omar. A regular human one, I might add!"

She explained that she couldn't go to work when she started feeling terribly sick because of the pregnancy and couldn't stop vomiting. She had left a letter with the school secretary to be read out to the class, but it must have been overlooked. So the conversation I overheard in the staff room was about a baby, not an alien.

The stack of mail had gathered because Mrs. H was away, but she was away *by choice*. She hadn't been abducted. The strange circles on her grass were from removing plant pots that had sat there for months, making the grass under them a different color.

I asked her about the alien-in-disguise creature. "We saw a really strange creature, though, that looked like an inside-out cat."

"Oh," Mrs. H chuckled. "That *is* a cat. My cat, Seb. I think he's cute, though I know hairless cats aren't everyone's cup of tea." She pulled out her phone and proudly showed us a picture of him.

"But what about the emails? Saying they saw you being taken by aliens?" I asked. A teeny, tiny part of me still believed I was right, and Mrs. H was hiding it all from us.

"I'm afraid somebody might have seen your posters and was pulling your leg, Omar."

"Oh . . ."

Mrs. H was touched, nonetheless. She couldn't believe her students cared about her so much.

"I did hate to be away from you all," she sighed.

I gave her a big hug. I know you don't really hug teachers, but here in Pakistan in these crazy circumstances, it felt like the right thing to do. I guess I hadn't imagined seeing her, but I had let my imagination make up a more exciting story from the clues we had found. Oops.

CHAPTER 25

I was allowed to call Charlie and Daniel to tell them everything that had happened. I sent them a message first to ask them to meet up so I could tell them together.

"That's the CRAZiEST STORY I ever heard! What are the chances?" said Charlie.

"Well, apparently better chances than her being taken by aliens," I admitted sheepishly.

"I *told* you guys it wasn't aliens!" said Daniel proudly.

"But what about those articles we read

about there being aliens out there?" Charlie asked.

"Well, Dad said they found life-forms, but that's not the same as actual green aliens that can walk and kidnap humans. It's just little bacteria or something puny like that."

"Oh . . . hahahaha."

"But who sent us those emails? I'll get them!" said Daniel.

Charlie's eyes went wide. "How can we not have guessed it? I bet it was Ellie and Sarah! They were always eavesdropping and asking questions!"

"Argh, I knew they were up to something!" I said.

"Hahaha, guess they got us this time!"

By the end of the conversation, we were in

hysterical fits of Laughter

about it all.

"I'll see you guys when I get back in a couple of days!" I said.

I was desperate to see them to talk more about it. On the plane, it was all I could think of, instead of watching movies or doing puzzles.

I thought about the dinner we had had the evening before we flew back home. Mom had arranged for us to have a proper meal with Mrs. Hutchinson and her husband. He was very nice and actually reminded me of Dad quite a lot. No wonder he was driving fast that day!

I thought about the time when I was new in class and nobody knew it was Ramadan, but Mrs. H did. I guessed it was probably because of him, which made me like him more.

When we finally arrived back at our front door, I was so happy. There's no place like your own home. Even though we had had lots of fun and had finally solved

Operation Moon Dust.

Mrs. Rogers was glad to have us back, too.

She loved all the gifts we got her:

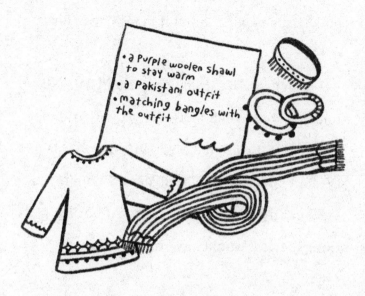

- a purple woolen shawl to stay warm
- a Pakistani outfit
- matching bangles with the outfit

I got Charlie and Daniel some stickers and

postcards with funny things written on them,

and some key chains that said,

I ♥ PAKISTAN

I even got Mrs. Crankshaw

a scarf, because Mom said

it would be **a nice gesture.**
On my first day back at school, I wrapped it in

pink tissue paper and put it in my bag to give

to her.

I didn't run in through the school gates like

I normally do when I haven't seen my friends

for a while. I was glad Mrs. Hutchinson was

OK, but still super sad that she wasn't our

teacher anymore. I wondered what boring

things Mrs. C would have in store for us

today.

I saw Daniel and Charlie doing the same sad

walk as I was to our line in the playground.

Though we cheered up a bit when I told them

both more about my adventure, especially the

car chase.

Daniel suddenly got a funny look on his

face. He quickly walked away and came back

with a stubborn-looking Sarah and Ellie. "Tell them," he said.

The girls looked like they had won and were very pleased with themselves. "It was us who sent you those emails, and we're sorry." They didn't *sound* sorry, not one bit.

"You'll be sorry when I make you eat avocados!" said Daniel.

Charlie and I laughed and put our arms around Daniel. "It's OK," we said. "It was funny, actually."

The bell rang and we all braced ourselves for another day with Mrs. CrankyForSure.

But when the teacher came out to get us, it wasn't her . . . it was Mrs. Hutchinson! In all her bouncy-hair glory!

The time away and some special medicines apparently made her feel a lot better, so she was able to come back and be our teacher again until her baby arrived.

It was the BEST DAY ever!

"Will you give Mrs. H the scarf instead?" asked Charlie.

I thought about it for a bit.

"No, I think Mrs. Crankshaw probably needs something to help her stop being so grumpy."

I smiled. "I'll mail it to her."

And I did.

TURN THE PAGE FOR A SNEAK PEEK
AT THE NEXT BOOK IN THE

SERIES!

ROARR

CHAPTER 1

RRRRRR!

The sound broke through the pin-drop silence of the classroom. It was the sound that was the start of the

WORST TWO WEEKS OF MY LIFE.

We were having a computer lesson, and my best friend Daniel couldn't wait to show me the new crazy video he had been talking about, of a lion being friends with a human and saving her from an attack by a hyena. I had said he could just email me the link and I would watch it at home, because I knew that our computer teacher, Mr. Philpot, would go absolutely bananas if he saw us.

But Daniel said, "No way. I can't live through the WHOLE day without showing you. It's only one minute long anyway."

And he hit the PLAY button with the sort of look on his face that my little brother, Esa, has when he's farted and he's waiting for everyone to smell it.

But it was the WOR$T idea possible, because:

- we are not allowed to watch videos in class.

- we forgot to plug in our headphones, so EVERYONE heard it.

- THE VOLUmE WAS ON (((FULL BLAST))).

Ellie even screamed and jumped out of her seat before she figured out it was just a video. I guess she thought a real lion had somehow come through the door.

Our other best friend, Charlie, was staring

at us from across the room, where he was

working with his partner, Adam.

HiS EYES
TRiPLED
iN SiZE.

Mr. Philpot was scanning the few

computers around us to make up his mind

who to shout at.

You haven't met Mr. Philpot before, so I will tell you about him. Remember Mrs. Crankshaw, the substitute teacher we once had instead of our lovely usual teacher, Mrs. Hutchinson? The really mean one? Well . . . Mr. Philpot made her look like a 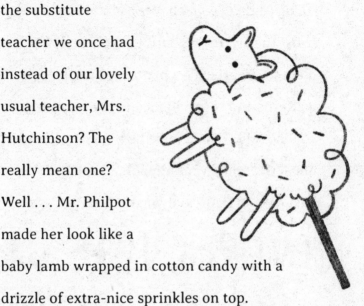 baby lamb wrapped in cotton candy with a drizzle of extra-nice sprinkles on top.

When Mr. Philpot shouted, you could hear him from the other side of the school building. And even if he wasn't shouting at you, you would still *shiver in your boots.*

The good thing was that it only happened

every so often, not all the time. I guess some things really made him blow his top, and other things didn't so much. We hadn't figured out what they were yet, but Charlie was on it. Because Charlie likes math so much, he sees patterns and common factors in everything, and he said, "There must be a common factor in all the times Mr. Philpot has exploded. We just have to figure out what it is so we

NEVER, EVER, like, EVERRRRRR do it."

But with the video, I thought we might have done it. I looked at Daniel and saw the horror in his eyes as Mr. Philpot took big fat steps toward us. Daniel used to be a mega-bullying

TROUBLEMAKER, but those

days are behind him. He hasn't been in trouble
for a long, long time, and I know how happy
that makes him. But now he would end up back
in the principal's office like he used to be ALL
the time before we were friends.

I saw a tear trickle down his cheek as he
put his hands on his ears to prepare for Mr.

Philpot's storm, and
I knew I had to do
something . . .

CHAPTER 2

I looked at Mr.

Philpot, who

was wearing his

usual shorts with

sandals. He had

knobby knees, and

something about

them made me imagine him as an ogre

covered in poisonous warts. This ogre

was about to eat my friend.

I stood up really fast. My legs felt all WOBBLY, but I found the courage to say,

"IT WAS ME!"

My hand went up to make super sure Mr. Philpot knew who to blame.

"You??" he said. He said it like he didn't believe it.

"Yes, me, sir. I did it; you can shout at me in my face, if you want."

That made somebody at the back giggle, but they quickly stopped when Mr. Philpot turned his poisonous warts toward them.

The whole class was looking at me.

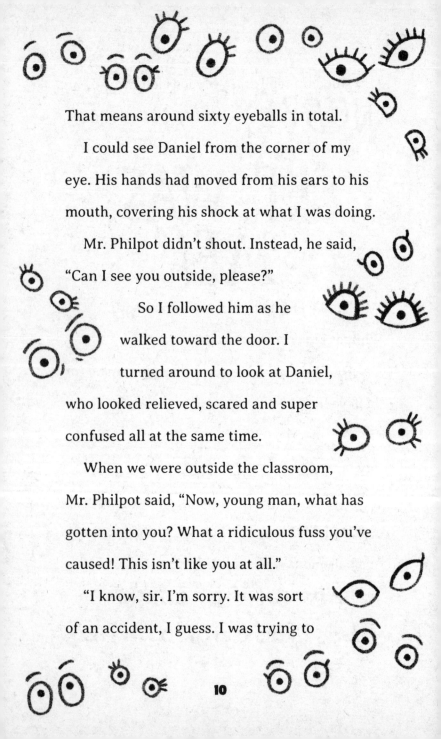

That means around sixty eyeballs in total.

I could see Daniel from the corner of my eye. His hands had moved from his ears to his mouth, covering his shock at what I was doing.

Mr. Philpot didn't shout. Instead, he said, "Can I see you outside, please?"

So I followed him as he walked toward the door. I turned around to look at Daniel, who looked relieved, scared and super confused all at the same time.

When we were outside the classroom, Mr. Philpot said, "Now, young man, what has gotten into you? What a ridiculous fuss you've caused! This isn't like you at all."

"I know, sir. I'm sorry. It was sort of an accident, I guess. I was trying to

catch my , which had

taken off into the air as if by magic, and ..."

I babbled on, trying to imagine ways a video

could be played by accident.

"OK. OK. Well, don't do it again, please, Omar.

You're a good kid."

And that's it! I was let off the hook. No principal's office, no earth-shattering shouting, no anything at all.

With a wide smile of relief, I walked back to my seat next to Daniel, who could still be Daniel-the-kid-who-used-to-be-a-troublemaker-but-is-now-a-totally-awesome-well-behaved-kid instead of Daniel-the-naughty-kid-who-has-gone-back-to-his-bad-ways. That made me feel

really super fantastic.

I had helped my friend and everything had turned out great.

When it was time for recess, the first thing Charlie said to me was,

"Omar, YOU aRE a hERO!"

Daniel said, "I can't believe you took the blame for me! It was so crazy! I always knew you were cool, but I never thought I would ever have a friend that cared so much he would get in TROUBLE for me."

OK, now

I felt awkward and shy because Daniel and Charlie were making it a big superhero deal. So I did a handstand to distract them. I had been practicing at home and had only broken one lamp in my mission to get really good (and the telling-off I had gotten from Dad was totally worth it).

It worked. Charlie and Daniel started clapping and trying to do their own

handstands,

which they weren't quite managing just yet.

Soon other kids from our class were coming up to me to ask what happened. And when they found out it wasn't really me who had played the lion video, but that I'd taken the blame so Daniel wouldn't get into trouble, they all looked at me as if I had burped a rainbow or something.

For the rest of
the day, I got

SPECIAL
tREAtMENt

from all the

kids in the class. The best things were:

• Sarah let me cut in front of her in the lunch line.

• Jayden gave me his Pokémon pencil.

• And Adam even asked if I wanted to play soccer with him, which he has never done in the history of my feet stepping into this school.

DON'T MISS OMAR'S
NEXT ADVENTURES!

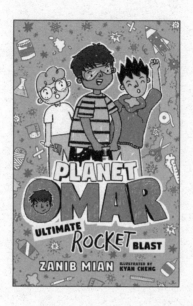

Can Omar's quick thinking and kind heart help his team work well together to build a winning rocket?

MAKE SURE YOU'VE READ
ALL OF OMAR'S BOOKS!